Tuesday, July 7th 2026

A week now since my cancer diagnosis and I'm just getting my head around having less than three years left to live, don't get me wrong, I always expected to die I am surprised I made my 50th birthday after all the follies of my misspent life, by follies I mean My former addiction to crack and other unsavory acts. Anyhow back to my death dairy, it's weird but when you get the diagnosis you expect the world to stop but the other 10 billion seem to be just getting on with life and although I am a practical man, my head and heart are screaming that it's not fair. Not a good day today, feeling shit and have a blinding headache, these sirens are not helping, it seems that every emergency service is working overtime this morning. The temp outside is 37c, apparently the 2nd hottest day we have experienced in England, it still seems weird having to refer to my home as England when I have always stated I am from the U.K but since the collapse of the government after the no-deal Brexit of 2019, Scotland devolved and joined the E.U, Ireland is now reunified and a member state of Europe but with U.N. troops keeping the peace, plus Wales is having a referendum, now we have an armed hard border on our island and England is becoming poorer and more isolated. Screw this, this weather is not helping, I am going to score some weed and draws the curtains.

Wednesday 8th July 2026

Slept almost the entire day away yesterday after I scored some nice bud, I was lucky to catch him in, the sirens of yesterday were because of a mob of homeless in the city (Derby) off their heads on the new synthetic drug of choice, were going around attacking and biting people, even my dealer got mixed up in the carnage and got a bite for his troubles, I told him he does not look good and to head for the hospital but knowing him, he will not bother. Feeling a bit better today, so pleased the weather broke and the temp has gone down, it is pissing down outside but still very muggy. Just looked out my window and saw Mick (my dealer) walking around without his shirt in the rain, he doesn't look too good, I'd better go check.

Not sure what is wrong with Mick but he seems to be in some sort of daze, I swear the guy did not even recognise me. I assumed he had been on the new drug because he came straight at me aggressively but soon as he got within feet he lost interest and stumbled away. Decision day for me, I have to decide how to move forward with treatment but I cannot see the logic of having invasive/ painful treatments that will only give me an extra few months. Pain relief is all I give a crap about and it might be nice having the state as my dealer. A nice walk with Max (my Shih Tzu) might help me clear my head. Early evening now and after a good walk, in which we did not see anyone, which is unusual. Not sure what the crack is but it seems that the new synthetic drug is causing issues across the country, there has been a report from London/Nottingham/Leeds and Newcastle of the homeless attacking and biting people. Would love to think it is a zombie outbreak but my imagination deserted me a long time ago. Can't be arsed to cook so I am ordering a Chinese and off to bed.

Thursday 9th July

Well, this started as my cancer diary but it seems that more important shit is going on at the moment, the news is full of the troubles, every city and some towns are experiencing attacks, they are no longer blaming the homeless or the new drug. It seems to be some sort of virus that is highly contagious, although not airborne, it is contracted via bodily fluids. London is suffering the worst and there is talk of calling in the army and initiating martial law. To be fair, the army might be a good idea since the new Protection officers replaced the police in 2023 were fucking scary, We have all heard the reports and seen the footage of the PO'S violating human rights and rounding up non-Christians and placing them in relocation camps (apparently for their protection) The coalition government consisting of the new E.N.P. and Britain first parties came into power within months of the great food riots of 2021 and are nothing but dirty fascist, ever since Tommy bloody Robinson became the new minister for internal affairs, this country is nothing more than a racist fascist state, certain that minister Robinson got done for fraud and contempt back in the day, the smarmy bastard. I am not even sure who is left in the commonwealth because countries seemed too distant themselves from us in the last few years, I know for certain Canada/Australia/ New Zealand and other obscure African countries have declared republics so far. I am going to spend the afternoon trolling the now restricted internet to see what exactly is going on.

Friday 10th July

Well after spending the afternoon surfing the web yesterday, I am very worried, not scared because I'm dying already but none the less very worried. I rang my sister in Nottingham and she said it is getting really bad, my nephew was bitten and is in the Q.M.C (queens medical Centre) apparently the hospital is full of new cases and are not coping well, Allison says that the protection officers are in force there and are armed. I wish I could tell her and my other sisters to move out of the city but where the fuck would they go. Unemployment has been at 60% of the population for over five years now and people can barely afford the foodstuffs that are still being imported. We have a population of 65 million in an area that homes grown produce and livestock can only support 10/14 million. Anyway, the net is full of videos of the carnage, they are biting/eating their victims, I know it sounds fucked up but we all saw the footage of a protection force van plough into a crowd in Newcastle and one of the infected lost the entire lower half of his body and still crawled toward an officer who escaped the van. The official line is that the infected are NOT dead but anyone who has viewed YouTube knows that is a load of bollocks. The Government has declared a curfew of 7 pm-7 am and banned travel outsides the cities, the army has cordoned off London and are going borough to borough shooting the infected, it may sound sick but I am shouting at the footage on TV telling them to use headshots, it is like all the sad zombie flicks where survivors shoot the infected in the chest/legs then get bit because the infected don't die (a second time). Tomorrow I am going into Derby city Centre to hopefully pick up some supplies.

Saturday 11th of July

Got up early today to hopefully miss the crowds in town, headed to town by 7.30 am but should not have worried about crowds, I have seen one person on the walk in, most of the shops are closed until further notice. Luckily Salisbury and Tesco are open as normal, although armed protection officers are guarding the entrance. Thank god I had squirrelled away money for a rainy day in the flat, the banks have stopped people withdrawing money because they have had a run on the banks? Like people even know what that means, I have managed to get some good supplies in, mainly dried goods and tins, nothing with a short shelf life. The crowds are out in force now but nothing compared to a usual Saturday, I hear the occasional scream and see the protection officers running towards them but besides that, it seems pretty normal. I am going to take the food home and then head back to town to collect a few things from the camping store.

Late afternoon and back in town, got a nice tent and a few bits like a flint striker and water purification tablets. There is a lot of talk about the army setting up camp at the holiday inn on Morledge near the bus station. I know I shouldn't but I am heading to the multi-story car park that overlooks the hotel to see what is happening. I thought the car park thing was a good idea but it looks like at least 50 people had the same idea, from here, there is a clear view of the army setting up a roadblock, not sure why though, screw this, I am heading to a lower floor to have a joint in peace, then head home.

Sunday 12th July

SHIT SHIT SHIT! Proper kicked off yesterday, whilst having a spliff in the car park I heard lots of shouting and screaming from the direction of the bus station, I headed back up to the top level to have a nose and now wished I had not. It was like a scene out of hell, several hundred infected were stumbling down moor edge from the ring road. At first, it looked like the army had their shit together and row after row of the infected fell. it was carnage but gave us all some hope, people were shouting and cheering them from the car park assuming that the battle was being won but then another group of maybe thousand came from the opposite direction.

It was a massacre, the army did not cover their backs and was swarmed by the mob, there is now no doubt whatsoever that the infected are truly the dead rising, I saw one loose both arms and a leg but still crawling towards the barricade. It was over in a matter of 10 minutes, the army (in derby at least) have now joined the new army of the undead, it seems unreal that two hours before I was shopping in Tesco around the corner.

Monday 13th July

Well, I made it home OK but it was crazy, they were everywhere, I had to dodge down a few sides streets, the weird thing is one of the fuckers had the drop on me and had every chance to have a nosh on my arm but she just totally ignored me. I have filled every decent container I have with tap water and sorted my food out if it does go tits up now, I know I can survive for at least a month. heard breaking glass last night, thank god I live on the second floor of my small block of flats, next door is vacant but both front windows of the flats downstairs are broken and it looks like the tenants have been either fled or joined the undead, there is a shuffling noise in the communal hall. I know what it is and I will have to deal with it I suppose, 999 is just an automated response now so no help there. Max is looking at me with his walkies eyes but scared to take him out. Right, hero time, got my biggest carving knife and heading into the hall,   well I was right about the noise, it is/was my neighbour Elaine, no fingers on her right hand at all and defo infected/dead. I thought I was being careful but as soon as I had got down most of the stairs, she turned around and faced me, I raise the knife and was ready to plunge it into her head but she just looked straight through me as if I was not there. I never liked the bitch but I figured that if she didn't attack, there was no point in spilling her brains unless I had to. I carefully moved around her and opened the main door to the street and held it open, my guess was right, she went straight out of the door and wandered off up the road. Luckily the back communal garden is fully enclosed with fences and the main gate, so I grabbed max and headed outside, I know max was not in danger because I had seen them totally ignored the army dogs and on the way home had also seen them disregard cats. Max seems happy to be out and is quite content lying in the sun. Another massive crash and I turn around to see the window of the flat next down come crashing out, followed by old Mr.'s Howarth, seeing a 70 years old lady falling out a second-floor window is not something I would recommend but seeing her get up with her head twisted at an unnatural angle is even worse. The fence between us is only about four foot but I knew she would never be able to get over it, so I decided to perform a little experiment, I went to my side of the fence and stood facing her, yet again she looked totally through me so I raise my hand to near her face (knowing that I was quicker than her) she just looked at my hand and turned the opposite way and stumbled off. If it was not for cancer, I would have felt like I had won the lottery, ME immune to the undead???

Tuesday 14th July

Not feeling great so decided that I will get stoned and find out all the information I could get from the net and TV. Yesterday after the episode with the neighbours, I decided to be brave and headed to Micks (my dealer). I knew he would not be there because I saw him last week and he was infected/dead.   I only saw a couple of the shambling wrecks on the way but yet again, they paid me no attention whatsoever. Thank god mick lives on the ground floor, his bathroom window was open because he has three dogs, I reached in and opened the main window, once opened I was greeted by three smiling animals, ok not smiling but I knew they liked me and have known me a few years. First thing first, I fed and watered the dogs then searched around. JACKPOT! Found at least 4 and a half ounces of good weed and some Charlie but not really into coke so I will keep that for a rainy day, I did not know what to do with the dogs, there was no way they were coming with me because Max fucking hated two of them. I decided to open the kitchen door and put out all the dry dog food I found and filled every container I could with water I don't think they will meet with much resistance in their future and will learn to thrive. I got back home with no problems and settled down to the news channel and internet. It is like watching some surreal horror movie, it turns out that the first cases were reported in NYC on the 4th/5th of July but no one figured how serious it was so intentional travel was not suspended, There has been no news from the east coast of America since Saturday, we are still getting news from Washington but it is muddled and not sure what to believe, it seems that the national guard has taken over the government and are issuing evacuation orders, Canada has closed its borders but has confirmed cases in Montreal and Toronto, Asia is virtually wiped out and the last news report from there is that India and Pakistan have launched nuclear missiles at each other, Beijing has fallen and the little news out of China seems to confirm that they have been overrun, Russia has been in a civil war for the past 18 months so no one is expecting any real news from them, although the staff of their embassy here have all claimed asylum to the British government. The Arab states are keeping their shit to themselves but NET rumour has it that Italy has nuked Libya to stem the influx of refugees carrying the virus. As for our Government, as of Friday last week, they and other self-important people were relocated to HMS Queen Elizabeth which is in the Irish sea, the rest of the fleet is scattered between the worlds hot spots, all overseas armed forces have been recalled, all air traffic (except military) have been suspended, there is the rumour that the government is going into hiding on the isle of man. No mention of the royal family at all which surprised me. Martial law is in effect in all counties plus all cell telecommunications had been commandeered for priority use and anyone outside their homes are liable to be detained or shot. London has gone, there has been no official news from them in 2 days and the blockade failed, there is talk of at least a million infected heading north down the M1/A1 corridors, on a positive note Tommy Robinson, our nasty little minister of the interior was bitten last week whilst visiting a relocation (detention) Centre for refugees in Luton. I know I should not think this but I hope it was a Muslim who bit the fucker. Most of Europe is infected now, no news from Germany for over 12 hours and Paris has fallen. New Zealand seems to be faring well, not one case reported yet but I heard they got their shit together early and banned planes landing, they effectively cut themselves off from the rest of the world. Australia fell within the first few days and what is left of their navy is now protecting New Zealand waters. It seems that the virus or whatever it is becomes dormant in freezing conditions, Iceland is doing well, I heard jersey and Guernsey were safe but it looks like refugees from the south of England got there and took the virus with them. I imagine that coastal towns were the only ones defying the non-travelling order because they could use the sea to escape. Proper tired now to going to build a fat one and sleep.

Wednesday 15th

I know this sounds proper odd but I have an appointment today with my probation officer (got caught with some weed a few months ago) So responsible citizen that I am, I will go, to be fair I know it is pointless but I figured that the dead do not want to hurt me, the desperate survivors might, I needed a weapon and at the weekend I saw the surviving army-run for their lives discarding their guns and ammo. The walk into town was really strange, so quiet. I took Max with me and if anyone alive had seen us they would have smiled, we must have looked odd. Had to pass the ring road in town and it looked normal either way, not what you would expect in an apocalypse but we are British and most would have obeyed the travelling ban, to be fair after Brexit if you didn't have an electric car or have a highly paid job, you don't drive in England. The city seems serene, I know that sounds fucked up but everything is virtually intact, lots of litter but other than that it's just at peace, even knowing the carnage on moorledge is just two streets away does not impede on the tranquility.

Plenty of cats about, not so many dogs though, I guess they mostly dead, trapped in their homes with their loved ones. I was chuffed I had released Mick's three dogs yesterday. I was right, I manage to pick up a rifle and two handguns with ammo, not sure how the rifle works and cannot Google the fucker because the net and phone coverage disappeared last night, part of me is pleased, don't get me wrong I love the net but I fucking hated social media that the nasty far-right used as their foundation to warp peoples mind and bring them to power. I got to probation and it looks intact but the doors are open, upon entering I realised something died in here, I take a peek through the inner security windows, I guess probation must have still been doing business as the first window I come to, I see my probation officer in an interview room trying to break the glass window with his head, he looks like she has been at it a while as there is a dried blood splodge on the window. I went in the main doors, it seems the phone lines are working so I will bell my family from reception, and not many people have landlines anymore except businesses and the over 50's. No reply from any of my sisters and my bro just has a mobile.

Heading back home, this shit has given me a blinding headache. Think I may have sussed why they are not interested in me, just saw a couple of local druggies on my way home, quite happily out their face and the dead are just ignoring them. Luckily I know one of them from my crack days so I went to chat. Seems they are loving life, all their drug dealers are dead so they took their stashes, plus all chemist shops available to them. I asked why the dead are not bothering them and Steve replied quite happily that the dead don't want to get aids from them. Three survivors, all of us with a life-threatening illness, cannot be a coincidence, can it?

Thursday 16th July

Electric has gone during the night, BBC radio Nottingham is still broadcasting thank god for the wind-up radio, but nothing else. Just want to have a spliff and think about things tomorrow. Seriously thought about that for a minute there but shit to do, I guess I have to think about moving on, I have to find a petrol car because electrics still do not have the range here in England. Darley Abbey is not that far, hope I can get in since it became a walled community. Got to sort out Max and my backpack and after Darley off we go to Nottingham to check on family and then to god knows where the dales are pretty remote but I was thinking more the Malvern Hills or wales. I was out of the flat within two hours of making the decisions, I could have stayed there a few weeks but it would just become like a tomb and I ain't dead yet.

Took max's harness and collar but not needed to attach the lead once, he just ignores the fuckers as they have always been part of his life, he has barked at one dog that was approaching but the thing ran off. Getting in Darley was no issue though as the gates were down. It looks like the battle for humanity took place in the suburbs, compared to the city this place is hell, bodies everywhere real dead ones, homes burnt out, car crashes but as I got further in, things seem semi-normal, I know there are a couple of new build around the corner that have walled gardens, hopefully, I should find a car there. Managed to get over the wall only to be confronted with a woman shakily pointing a shotgun at me, thank god she has got her practical head-on, she has not shot because rightly so, she explained the infected cannot climb, I explained who I am and asked if she could open the security gates a tiny bit just to let Max in, I think the dog clinched it, what kind of robber would have a Shih Tzu in tow? After introducing myself and Max we were invited in and exchanged stories. Her name is Rebecca and she is 34, quite attractive if you're into a woman but luckily I'm not so no issues there.

This is/was her dad's house, apparently some big wig in the east midlands chapter of the E.N.P. They were supposed to be airlifted to the aircraft carrier at the weekend but no helicopter turned up, neither of them is ill (infected or otherwise) and she seems to be a genuine survivor, her dad went off yesterday in the range rover to a wholesale food outlet near east midlands airport but has not returned yet, apparently, he is a survival nut and has lists after lists of wholesalers and food stores in England. Not impressed with her dad being a party official but bite my tongue, luckily she was very forthcoming about her political views and happily described her dad as a bigot and racist. I think we are going to get on. After a long chat, we have decided that I should stay the night and we both head toward east midlands airport in the morning.

We had a pleasant night, they have the new solar power panels that generate enough power to run a big home, so we sat down to a nice roast beef dinner with all the trimming plus two bottles of very expensive wine, it turns out that Rebecca has not grasped the full scale of the crisis and has stayed protected in her walled luxury home in the walled community. I filled her in as best I could then went into the garden to roll a spliff. Surprisingly Rebecca joined me and was quite happy to have a few tokes on the joint.

We went back in to try the TV but No one is broadcasting so we switched on the radio, There were only two broadcasts, one was radio Nottingham and the other was some random god squad guy ranting about how we brought this on ourselves and that the dead are walking because hell is full. I hope that if there are groups of survivors that they will not be chained down by religious dogma, hopefully, world religions end here and the Christian/Muslim god goes the same way as Nordic/roman and Greek gods. Radio Nottingham is painting a pretty dismal picture of the situation over there, It has described the carnage in all the suburbs with rioters and the undead blurring into one and the infection spreading at an amazing rate, there are two sets of survivors, one based at the Queens medical Centre and another holed up in the castle, I'm assuming the group at the hospital are people that were already seriously ill so were not attacked by the infected. There are a few hundred hiding out at the castle, all they had to do was barricade two 15 fete wrought iron gates and the rest is defended by its wall and the sandstone cliff, There was trouble there a few days ago when the protection officers ordered all the people of colour and different religions out on the premise that white British people would have more supplies,   luckily the army stood up to the bastards and after a few shots were fired the protection officers backed down, the army ordered all the protection officers to leave and not return, never thought I would say this but thank fuck for the army.

Friday 17th July

Had a good night's sleep, Rebecca offered me her dads bedroom which was opulent, to say the least, for god sake, who has a bar in the bedroom? We are setting out today to the wholesalers near east midlands airport officially to find her dad, not that I give a toss what happened to him but I figure some supplies might be nice, this whole Apocalypse thing has not fazed me, don't get me wrong I am worried about my family in Nottingham but besides that, I have no one(by choice) I am a bit of a loner and I enjoy my life without the trimmings of society, not that society in England is that great since Brexit. Gay people/Muslims/Jews and ethnic minorities have not had it great in the last few years, We are being openly discriminated against since the far-right came into power, they have made it obvious that we should keep a low profile, the last London pride almost four years ago ended in a riot because the government granted permission for one of their far-right Christian marches on the same day, over 50 dead in total, 28 were far-right, so it was the perfect excuse to ban further pride events. Every day on the Euro news channel we were watching attacks on minority groups in our country, although the new E.B.C tried to give us the real news the government took over all our channels and appointed commissionaires to oversee what was broadcasted. Of course, we had the net but the government censored most sites and banned others. It was pretty easy to bypass their bans thanks to V.P.N (a virtual private network). England has become a worldwide embarrassment and there are very few western countries willing to trade with us because we violate people's human rights constantly. We were going to walk into town to try to get some transport, perhaps a decent van or something to carry supplies back. As soon as we opened the gate the dead started approaching us, I did not realise at first why because they have ignored me previously, then I realised that Rebecca is not immune to these things. We promptly went back in and secured the gate. the new plan is that I head out to find a suitable vehicle then come back, I decided to leave Max with Rebecca then headed for town, Not entirely sure where I can find a vehicle but will have a good look around, Plenty of the dead about today, I guess they just roam at random now, I did see two army lorries headed towards the ring road but decided not to make my presence known for now.

Just thought of a place to find a van, the old industrial estate near Pentagon Island has several new and used commercial vehicles dealers and if I remember rightly they have their petrol pumps outback, Got to the dealerships pretty easily and found a nice transit van, although not new it would fit the bill nicely. On the way back to Rebecca, I decided to check the A52 to see if there would be a later issue with traffic. People did obey the no travelling order, I guess they were scared to go anywhere because of the penalties that the government issued. Not one car on the A52 so headed to junction 25 of the M1, I stopped on the bridge overlooking both carriageways and it seemed clear for miles in both directions, there was a convoy of army trucks headed north that had stopped whilst one of the trucks was having a wheel replaced. I headed down to them to see what the crack is. I approached them with my hands in the air and was permitted to talk to one of their senior offices, it seems that they came from a safe zone near Luton that fell a few days ago, at least five of their trucks have survivors and the rest(ten in all) are fully loaded with supplies.

They are headed up to the border country than to Scotland there is a community of survivor's near-eye mouth in a walled community that generates its own green energy and has a natural water source. The survivors in the trucks were allowed off to stretch their legs and I was happy to see at least half of them were ethnic minorities, a few laid their prayer mats on the tarmac and began to pray, no one batted an eyelid and it made me for the first time in years to be proud to be English. It seems that lots of survivors are former inmates of the government's relocation centers. When the world was going to shit, these people were behind high-security fences so avoided the worst of the troubles. The officer I spoke to told me that a relocation camp in Northampton was overrun by the inmates and all the protection officers were given a stark choice of staying and contributing to the group or leaving, apparently most left but that is not surprising as the main skill you needed to become a protection officer was to be a small-minded bigoted wanker.

I stayed for a while but before I left, I asked if one of them was willing to come to the derby with me to pick up some of the paperwork that has lists of the food distribution centers on their way, one of the former inmates from the camp approached and explained that he was never bitten even when he was in a no-win situation with the dead and that he would come with me because they were not interested in him, he introduced himself as Jamal and he seems like a nice bloke, I was about to ask if he was ill but he beat me to the punch and explained that the dead are not attacking people with serious illnesses, it seems that the army is also aware of this trait and has stopped at several hospitals rescuing survivors. The convoy will still head north but at a much slower pace until Jamal returns, we set off me in the van and Jamal following in an electric car, I should not have worried about the distance the electric car can travel because the army officer explained that there are charging stations all over the country with the new solar panels that can charge a car to full in 20 mins.

Nothing exciting on the journey and we were back to Rebecca in half an hour, Max greeted me like I had been gone years and took well to Jamal. After a quick bite to eat We gave Jamal a few copies of the paperwork and wished him well on his journey, I did ask Rebecca if she wanted to join him but she was adamant that she find out what happened to her dad. It was now late in the day so we decided to head off the next morning.

Saturday 18th July

We set off very early the next morning and made it to east mids airport in 25 mins, there was a battle here as we saw hundreds of the undead(now dead) lying around the main gate, we saw army machine gun posts now overran by the horde. The battle must have been a few days ago because there were hundreds of flies around the bodies but very few maggots and I am certain that maggots only eat for a few days before reaching larva development and become flies. Whilst I was mesmerised by the carnage, I saw Rebecca run toward an upturned range rover and suddenly she screamed, I took out my pistol and rushed over assuming there was danger but I found Rebecca on her knees crying over the struggling undead still in the driving seat trapped by a seat belt. It did not take a genius to realise who the driver was and knelt beside her to offer some comfort, after a few minutes, Rebecca asked if she could use the gun, I promptly passed it over and walked away towards the open gate. After a few minutes, I heard a shot and Rebecca joined me, there was no need for an explanation as I know for certain that if I discovered my loved ones in that state, I would put a bullet in their brains too.

The gunshot must have alerted someone as we heard shouts coming from the airport grounds, we left the vehicles and walked into the compound, we saw one or two stumbling wrecks in the distance but figured that we had time to escape if they came close, after having a look around we noticed several people on the control tower balcony waving to us. We head straight to them and suddenly the door to the tower was thrown open and two soldiers beckoned us in. inside there was a group of seven, three army and two civilians and a child, we were offered a hot drink and settled down to hear their story, apparently the airport was being used to transfer bigwigs and their families to the isle of man but normal civilians turned up at the gates in their hundreds, the infection came with them and spread so fast that the army could not deal with the numbers, The last helicopter left four days ago and of the 50 or so army personnel and 20 civilians left behind, these were all that was left. We told how the story and I explained about the survivors I met heading north on the M1, there was obvious relief on their part that they were not the only survivors. After an hour or so and a bite to eat, it was decided that they and Rebecca would head towards the M1 and hopefully catch up with the convoy, luckily the senior officer I had met had told me their route north after Leeds so there should be no issues, the survivors told me that transport was not an issue as there were several fully loaded lorries with food stores at the wholesalers in the industrial estate about a half-mile away and they had their diesel depot too. I went back to the lorry and drove it to the tower to collect the survivors and transport them to the industrial estate, Rebecca joined me in the cab and on the way she kindly offered to take Max with her, I know it sounds selfish but I have had Max from nine weeks old and could not imagine him not being with me, Max is a happy little boy and seems quite content in this new world with all, the new smells and exciting new places, I declined Rebecca's offer and dropped off the survivors in the estate, Luckily the food store and diesel plant were all in the same walled complex so we had to do was secure the gate and then take time to fill up the tanks.

As I was about to head off Rebecca rushed to me and gave me the biggest hug and the keys to her home in derby, explaining that with the power still on there and the wall, it would be a good place to fall back on if things went tits up, I happily took the keys and headed off, I did think of heading straight to Nottingham but decided that a nice hot bath and a few drinks in a secure place would do me the world of good, plus I still had micks weed. I drove through Melbourne on the way back and although there were signs of damage, it all looked pretty normal, I passed a small shop on the way that was intact except for an open door and decided that I could grab some dog food and cigarette and Rizal papers. I pulled up and headed into the store, there was obviously a fight near the till and a rotten body lay there, the smell was awful, I went further into the store but the shelves were virtually empty, it seems that people in the rural towns had time to loot before the infection reached them, whilst in the city people, although afraid of the infected were more terrified of the armed protection officers, there were reports in the early stages of the outbreak from London and other southern cities of officers shooting infected and non-infected alike.

Now, this is the surrealist part of my story, from a few gardens away, I heard a woman voice shout "afternoon dear, I wonder if you could help me". I looked towards the sound and saw a woman who must have been in her 80's kneeling down in her garden picking carrots, I approached and asked her what was wrong and she told me that nothing was wrong but could I please help her up because her knees were not what they were. This made me smile, I helped her rise and she offered me into her home, she introduced herself as Edith and offered me a drink, after a cup of tea she explained what happened in Melbourne.

She told me that things were normal for a few days after the reports on TV about the infected but when helicopters and planes started arriving at the airport most people from the town headed there hoping for evacuation and never came back so she assumed they have got out of the area. She told me that although there were still a very few left in the town that they kept themselves to themselves, apparently she had seen some of the infected roaming around but they paid her no attention whatsoever so she carried on as normal, I knew the reason they were ignoring her and what happened to her friends and neighbours but she was such a sweet old dear that I did not have the heart to tell her.

I asked her how she still had electricity and she explained that she had those new-fangled solar panels on the roof and most of the town got their electricity from the wind turbines a few miles north near derby. I did explain to her what I knew of the situation and offered her a ride to the convoy heading north but she was adamant that this has been her own for 87 years and she fully intended to die here. I could not argue with her and to be fair, I was a bit relieved because I did not want to drive miles away then double back to head to

Nottingham. After saying my goodbyes to Edith I headed back to Derby.

Sunday 19th July

Got shit faced last night after finding a nice single malt in the bar at Rebecca's house, slept in until 10 am and figured it's allowed on a Sunday, although every day is as quiet as Sundays nowadays. I stopped off in the city center yesterday to pick up a few essential items such as dog food and Rizal papers, no point in having weed unless you can make a blunt. After having a bite and feeding Max, we headed off to Nottingham on the A52, not looking forward to today but it has to be done, no problems on the drive until we reached junction 25 of the M1, I had to stop the van on the bridge because I could not believe my eyes, there must have been tens of thousands, probably hundreds of thousands stumbling infected on the southbound carriageway headed north, seems odd that none had crossed the central reservation to use the northbound. I wondered where they were heading to or were they just randomly roaming, the smell was awful like an open sewer pipe but much more intense, I carried on down the A52 until I reached the Q.M.C. surprisingly there was plenty of human activity here, several lorries were being loaded by a few dozen men and women. I parked up on the main drag and headed towards them on foot, as soon as I was within ten feet a shot rang out and the windscreen of a car immediately to my left exploded. I stopped dead and raised my hands in submission after a few words were exchanged I approached the nearest group and although cautious, they were very friendly, it seems that they have been camped out here since the initial outbreak but food and water were becoming an issue so they contacted the other group in the castle and have decided to pool resources, I explained that I had come to Nott's to hopefully find surviving family members. After helping them load for an hour or so, I decided to head to Broxtowe to hopefully find family members, I expected to see some roads blocked with traffic but even in a city the size of Nottingham, those who could afford to run a car had stayed at home. I know this sounds odd but people (including myself) were more scared of the protection officers and did not travel at all. on the three-mile trip to Broxtowe, things seemed semi-normal, there were a few bodies in the streets and several hundred infected roaming about but these things were now the norm and I very rarely looked at them. There were a few houses that had been invaded by the infected but for every house that had been damaged, there were five that had not. I got to Broxtowe but could not drive into the estate, no matter what entrance I tried to use there was an old barricade blocking the roads, not sure why but it looks like the protection officers had cordoned off the entire estate. I left the vehicle on Aspley lane and managed to get into the estate via the back gardens of a few houses, one in the estate things seemed pretty normal except for a few front windows broken and of course the bodies (both dead and walking) It looks like the barricades were not put up by the protection officers but by the people in the estate themselves, probably to cut themselves off from the infected but they were inside the barrier already. I walked through the estate to reach Lindfield road and I approached my sister's house, the windows were intact but the front room one was smeared with blood from the inside, My heart sank because that could only mean one thing, I entered the garden and started shouting my families names, no way was I going inside until I knew what was in there, after a minute or so several easily recognised faces appeared at the window but they were no longer my family though. Throughout this whole end of the world shit nothing had affected me probably because the infected left me alone and I have not had to fight for my life but this caused the worst pain I have ever felt, way back in 94 when I watched our mum take her last breath and her lips and fingertips turn blue I decided that nothing could ever hurt that bad again but I was so wrong, I could not stand anymore and virtually collapsed on the grass, crying like a baby.

Monday 20th July

After seeing my family yesterday, I headed back to the lorry via several streets where many of my extended family lived and the scenario was the same except for my youngest sister Wendy's home, it was intact and the curtains were closed, I went up and tried the door but it looks as if the house is fully locked up. I had no idea where they had gone but my greatest wish was that they had made it away from the city. I now had no idea what to do with myself, I had met my self-imposed moral obligations to the people I love/loved and to be fair I was so focused on that one mission that apart from thinking of leaving the cities far behind me, I had no real plans. As we got near the lorry max started barking at a figure standing near the cab, I realised that he must be alive because even though Max had raised a few barks towards the infected he gave up even noticing them a long time ago it seemed, even though two weeks ago things were normal. I shouted to the person asking him if everything was ok, they turned to face me and it was a bloke about 35 with a beanie on, now I'm not saying I am Sherlock or anything but a Beanie on in a hot July morning told me plenty, He introduced himself as Jack and seemed genuinely happy to see another person, as I was but still cautious/paranoid. Max loved him and ran straight up to him to get his strokes in, I know Max and I know he is a brilliant judge of character so that put me at ease and rightly so, Jack turned out to be decent. After the introduction, Jack was happy to tell me his story of survival. He was in the hospital when it proper hit the fan having chemo.   The hospital must have been the brunt of things because he fled there in terror on the 13th after nurses started biting/eating his fellow patients, since then he has been holed up in his mum's home on Sherbourne road. His mum was not there and the fact that she is/was a nurse told him that she was not coming back. The electricity lasted longer in Nottingham and the power only went off four days ago, except of course for all the new builds that filled in the green spaces between here and Derby. It became law three years ago that all new homes had to have an alternative energy source be that solar or wind power from the tens of thousands of turbines that cover most rural areas. The poor lad knew that the infected were not interested in him so he was free to enter homes and shops for foodstuffs, I was surprised that not many shops were looted in the early days but yet again even non-law abiding were as scared as the rest of us regarding the protection officers, I'm tempted to get all political now but any English person knows exactly what I mean. Anyway back to Jack, he did not stay at the hospital long enough to realise that the seriously ill were not at risk. I told him what I knew of the hospital lot and the fact that they were going to the castle, he picked up a bit on hearing this, explaining that he had made some real friends in his ward and the fact that they were like him, still alive proper brought a smile to his face, I know it's probably not the right time but I asked him if he smoked bud, to be fair he lived on Sherbourne in a rough estate and it was a high percentage was he did. His smile got wider and asked if I had any, we went back to his mums and to be fair we got mash-up big time (stoned to non-tokers) He had a nice bottle of single malt that his mum has had since his birth, a gift from his Irish uncle. He invited me to stay for the night, his mum had the basic solar panels so nothing but the fridge/cooker and a couple of lights were working, today has been my best yet since it all went to pot (pardon the pun). Jack is a top bloke, he explained he is well into his chemo but now it has stopped forever, he expects months rather than years but he was not sad about it, for both of us we are facing death for certain and instead of thinking that the world will just carry on after our death, the world seems to have died whilst we could get stoned and carry on. These are my words, jack or anyone one else may not think as cynical as me.

Tuesday 21st July

After a really good breakfast supplied by Jack, we headed to the castle in the city Centre, as before all the roads were still clear of traffic except for the A610 but even then there were very few vehicles but all had been shunted to the sides, we saw a couple of army vehicles heading out so I flashed my lights and pulled up, the lead lorry stopped but they did not get out and I realised why, there were several infected heading their way, I went up to the lorry and a middle-aged guy wound down his window, I asked about the castle and where they were heading, they were from the castle but were heading out to several local industrial estates looking for food supplies because the survivors from the castle were heading out of the city in the next few days because of fears of disease and need a freshwater supply. I told him to hang on a second whilst I went back to my lorry and fetched him a bunch of the print outs of food suppliers that I liberated from Rebecca's dads home. He thanked me and explained how helpful they were. The infected were now feet away and the guy was getting nervous, he knew that they were not bothering me but was decent enough not to mention it. I went back to Jack in the lorry and continued to the castle, as we approached the side 15ft wrought iron gates, I noticed that they had boarded off the insides of the railings with MDF or hardwood. There were a few infected around but as we neared the gate it was opened for us. We entered what seemed to be organised Chaos, everyone was busy packing vans and to my surprise, there were three Nottingham city transport buses, the new all-electric ones that could be charged within three hours and carry a charge for up to 1000 miles. As soon as we entered we were approached by a woman with a clipboard, she introduced herself as Jillian and as the official record keeper, she took our names/former professions and addresses then let us on our way but not before I gave the name of my youngest sister Wendy and her family and asked her to check to see if they had passed this way. Jack saw a few buddies from the hospital and after making me promise that I would not leave before saying goodbye made his way to them. I went straight to a group of soldiers having a smoke and asked about what they knew. It seems the army kept their act together and after the not few disasters of units facing the infected and being wiped out, they decided defense not offence was the way to go, one guy explained that most of the south beyond Northampton was now a dead zone, they have had no radio contact with anyone from there at all, most people that had escaped the cities which were piddling in comparison to the population headed out to walled communities which were now dotted everywhere in the countryside or to the relocation camps for what the government decided were undesirables, such as Muslims/Jews/Hindu's/gays/lesbians and roman travelers no one had any idea where they would be located to of course and If society had not collapsed god knows what would have become of them. The people of the camps welcomed their fellow survivors with open arms, including protection officers who had by now shed their racism. The army it seems is well organised and are actively feeding many of these communities and have set up communications with most of them. It seems that the infected areas stupid as I thought if you had a decent high fence around any properties, al, you had to was obscure their view inside with anything from curtains to wood and when the infected met a barrier where they could not see beyond they would just turn around and head off until they met another obstacle. This explained why many houses were still intact in the city, the homes with the curtains open and living inside and visible were mobbed but homes with curtains closed were bypassed by the infected. God! There could be millions of non-infected still living in the cities if they had enough water and supplies. There were very few infected in the countryside because after the food riots of 21 most company farms and a hell of a lot of villages decided to fortify their lands, with the villages it was as simple as gating the roads in and out because the surrounding fields were already fortified. They estimate that the entire population is now roughly just short of three million, I was shocked by this because that means over 60 million had succumbed to infection or death (walking or otherwise). I told them about my experiences and the fate of the army units in Derby on the 11th. One more piece of info that I imagine was supposed to be hushed was blurted out by a young soldier, that the rumour was that the government in hiding had fallen shortly after taking up residence of the Isle of Man. I smiled slightly at this and it was noticed and I expected anger but it seems they felt the same way I did. There is a meeting tomorrow about these communities' plans and where they are heading. I am going to stay the night but still unsure if I will join them.

Wednesday 22nd July

The meeting started at 9 am prompt, there must have been over 2000 people here after the hospital lot arrived last night and it was obvious there were too many to carry on here in the city, there are already a few cases of typhoid but with the raided medical supplies they were doing well. The plan is to head west to St David's in wales what's left of the navy and army had secured Anglesey/ ST David's and St Asaph in wales and have the electricity and water running, These were out of the way small cities that used 100% green energy from the wind farms off the coast in the Irish sea. I know it sounds daunting that we have just escaped a fascist government to be lead basically by a military one but we are assured that the only goal of the armed forces is to protect and serve the remaining population. We were also assured that the forces would not tolerate any of the previous governments policies on racism/gender and so on and looking directly at a group of 20 or so men stated that if anyone did not like this, they were free to leave, it was obvious to everyone they were former protection officers, he went on to say that this could be a new start and all were welcome regardless of their skin colour/religion or sexual orientation. This made me breathe a deep sigh of relief because no way was I even thinking of joining them if they continued with the hate that has dogged our country for the last decade. The speaker asked how many in the audience were immune to the infected, which of course meant how many were suffering from severe illnesses. at least 400 people raised their hands and the speaker explained that the combined forces had several hundred doctors and nurses and once the hospitals were up and running, we would receive specialist care including chemo and so on but in the meantime, we were their greatest assets as we could go out and take what was needed from the dead cities for the new communities, this gave me some sense of self-worth, something I had not had in a while and there and then I decided to stay with these people. The meeting went on for several hours and towards the end, I noticed that Max had left my side and headed towards the speaker who had a black Labrador with him, Max instantly tried to mount the bitch but as you know Max is a Shih Tzu and this brought instant laughter to the audience. the plan was to leave late this afternoon but first they needed some more transport, I knew where the bus depot was in Nottingham so I and a few other volunteered to head over and get a few other buses, it would take a while to charge them but I also knew the depot had a wind power turbine and the new industrial solar panels. We headed straight out as the depot was in Sneinton which by foot was a couple of miles on the other side of the city, we had to leave some volunteers behind because they were not immune. there were several hundred infected on the way but they did not bother us and within hours we were back to the castle, there was one more stop I needed to make in the city and Jack came with me, we headed to the library and found as many books we could on basic farming and raising cattle, I know nothing about such things and I am guessing most other city dwellers were as ignorant as me, I was hoping they may not be needed because the fortified farms were secured and the people there knew such things but you never know. As soon as we got back we were on the road again, this time in a convoy of five double-deckers at least 30 Lorries and a mismatch of vehicles ranging from land rovers to several electric motorbikes.

Thursday 23rd July

The journey was pretty uneventful except for a large   group of infected on the M4 numbering a few thousand, they were easily avoided though, I noticed this before, they were only using one side of the carriageway and not one ventured over the central reservation, all we had to do was double back to the last junction and use the opposite carriageway, as we entered Wales we noticed a fairly big walled estate just off the main road but with armed guards stationed in look out towers, two of the army lorries veered off towards them, the rest of the convoy carried on, after about an hour the two lorries rejoined the convoy, I flipped on the CB radio   that were fitted to every vehicle in the convoy, it seemed odd using technology that was around in the late forties onwards but it was a good way to communicate, I switched on ch14 and heard the returning soldiers explain that the entire community was made up of protection officers and their families and they stated that they had been watching the convoy for the last few miles and wanted nothing to do with people that could taint their future white blood lines, I guess having Asians and black people really stirred them up. The armies view was that they have a right to their views but wanted nothing more to do with them, but before leaving they explained on a loud hailer outside the gates, who we were, our views and destination and that if anyone changed their mind they were free to join us in the future. We arrived at St David's around 9 in the evening and were met by a fairly large group of soldiers who had cleared out at least a third of the city and secured it from the infected, in the coming days I imagined we the sick would join in clearing the rest, ST David's was a very small city of only a few thousand so it would not too great a job.

Friday 24th July

Rough night, I heard several high pitched screams from a few streets away, even though I was immune there was no way I was heading out into the night in a strange city but found it difficult to sleep. I headed out first thing to the makeshift canteen in the cathedral and took my fill of bacon and eggs but also to catch up on the nights' events, it seems that a family of poor souls had hidden in their loft but one of them must have been bitten because during the night they had fallen through the ceiling straight into the arms of a group of female army officers who had set up home there, we lost two to the infected but because they were army the rest contained the situation, there were two meetings later today, one for the non-immune civilians and another for the army but including the sick, it was obvious what the second one was about and although I understood we were needed, I was not looking forward to killing the infected even though I knew they were already dead. The first meeting was pretty standard about what we can expect from the army and what they expected from us, also telling people about last night and that if anyone should come across any infected in the safe zone, they were not to confront them but to run and report it to the army which was stationed in one house per street. the second meeting was what I feared it to be, there were well over a couple of thousand army personnel and at least 700 or so sick people, the army had picked up a few hundred on their way, after chatting to several I realised that cancer was the main cause of survival in our group, although there were quite a few with the HIV and other serious illnesses, the HIV patients were told that there was enough supply of the drugs to last years and they had many professional chemists who assured them the drugs were not difficult to manufacture, they could lead a normal life. The treatment in the last few years had improved greatly and people no longer died from AIDS but rather lived with HIV. The prognosis for aggressive cancer sufferers was not great, it would take some time for the hospitals to be up and running and to raid other cities for drugs but they would get there, the hospitals it seems were the first to be overrun, and once the population of the wards became infected, the pharmacies were left untouched. We were to accompany the army who were going street to street clearing the area from infected, our job was to enter homes and check every nook and cranny for them and either kill them or draw them outside for the army to finish the job. This work was to commence immediately so the meeting dispersed and we were allocated units to join, I saw Jack in the crowd and joined his group before heading out. There were plenty of infected about and the army took them out very professionally, the remains were thrown into the councils electric bin lorries and taken away to be burnt, one good thing about our former government is because most of the world would not trade with us that our country had to become self-sufficient in our daily lives, which meant for us green energy, most councils had switched to green electricity in the last few years so the infrastructure was there for us to begin again, although only sections of the big cities had green energy so far, there were even several thousand windmills scattered around the countryside, I dread to think how survival would be possible if we had to rely on fossil fuels even in wales where coal was still in abundance. Once the army had cleared a street they used their lorry to block the road and then it was our turn to go door to door, most doors were locked and our remit was to cause as little damage as possible because the living would be moving in, the first few houses were empty which I found odd because there was nowhere to run to and I imagine most died in their homes, after about six houses I entered a living room to find a family of six, two adults and four children, my method of dispatch was a heavy-duty screwdriver, I know that sounds odd but unlike the army, I could get in close and push the weapon into their eyes, unlike the films the dead do not bleed and this was a fairly simple way to dispatch them without their innards spilling out. the parents were first to go and they just stood there whilst I pierced their eye sockets, for the kids I had to kneel to their height and repeat the method, I was worried that I could not do the children but the infected are now a dark grey colour with glazed over eyes and seem as far from humans as can be. The day went pretty smoothly and I realised that the empty houses were not the norm, in many we found couples in bed, some with children, not infected but none the less dead, it seems many people who were too afraid to leave their homes from fear of either the dead or protection officers and took the brave way out. After clearing a few streets we came across a nursery with its gates firmly padlocked, outside there were several dead bodies, not dead as in walking but dead as in being shot but inside the gates were several dozen children all infected and a couple of halves eaten adults. I can only guess that the infection was discovered in the school and the protection officers locked the gates, the dead outside the gates were all fairly young adults and I imagine they were parents desperately trying to reach their young. The army shot all the visible children then it was our turn, the three classrooms were empty but we heard noises coming from the kitchen/small canteen. The door was barred from the inside and I could hear whispering coming from inside, I shouted out who we were and in reply,

I heard several gasps of breath, after a hurried conversation through the doors I explained that before they come out that we would check everywhere within the grounds of the nursery. We only found two other children, both infected but one of them was stuck on the tyre swing in the play area and from a distance, he could have been a carefree youngster playing. We went back to the door and explained it was all clear, the door eventually opened after they had removed the barricade, two young ladies followed by five young children, two boys and three girls, it seems that a child had come to school with a bite mark that he had received on his way to school, for whatever reason, his dad had not disclosed it to the teachers or took the lad for medical attention, by lunch the same day, the boy had turned and bit several classmates who in turn infected others, the teachers had managed to contact the protection officers before securing themselves in the canteen about two weeks ago, they survived because there was quite a lot of food stocks as they offered breakfast and lunch to underprivileged kids, water was becoming an issue as the taps stopped over a week ago but one of the teachers had the foresight to fill every container possible beforehand, I tried a tap and as the army had promised there was now a water supply again. The kids looked a bit dirty but other than that they were full of beans and had seen this as an adventure, luckily the teachers were wise enough not to let their fears spill onto the children's psyche. I radioed the army and told them we had found survivors and you could hear the joy in their voices when telling us a vehicle would be there within minutes, we made our way out of the school to the cheering of at least 50 army personal who had rushed to the site. After loading them up we decided to call it a day and headed to the safe zone. When we arrived there were hundreds of people waiting to greet us, and of course Max and his new partner in crime Minnie the black Labrador. as the kids were unloaded both dogs heading straight to them and started licking them, the kids were all smiles and happily took to the dogs, I know it sounds odd but I think the dogs knew these kids needed a bit of loving.

Friday, August 14th

I was planning to update this diary every day but the last few weeks have taken its toll, as well as clearing St David's, I have been volunteering for city runs to get much-needed supplies. I have not kept count but I have dispatched hundreds of the infected so far, I really thought I could handle it but the nightmares and stress have been horrendous, to make matters worse Jack who I met in Broxtowe Nottingham passed last night from his cancer, we became firm friends over the last few weeks as we both had the same background, I feel as if my last link to the old world has gone, He was cheerful to the end and it was an enormous pleasure to know the guy,   a unit of the army dealing with the disposal of dead were a bit insensitive and wanted to burn him with the infected but no way was I having that shit, luckily the units we were working for felt the same way and demanded that Jack had a real funeral, everyone liked Jack, he had a shine to him and always made people smile, we buried him yesterday in a local church yard and there must have been well over a hundred people attending, it was not a morbid event and many people spoke of how Jack had helped them with his upbeat personality even in times like this. I ended up crying like a baby, I was never afraid to show my emotions and I realised that I was not crying solely for Jack but also for my family and the millions who had succumbed to infection. We have almost cleared St David's now and the tension/stress has eased a little, I know this is not the ideal situation for romance but I have become very close to a Captain in the army called Jono who I have been working with, we have only kissed so far but there is chemistry there, others have noticed and we have been the brunt of several good-humoured banter, I expected some kind of abuse but everyone has been positive about us. From the beginning I expected the Army to be on a par with our last government but these people have been peacekeepers in many parts of the world including England over the last decade and a few explained that they had witnessed too much death and destruction from intolerance and bigotry and they were not about to initiate that shit again, I have to admit that I have misjudged the army, I thought at first that they were just organised thugs for the government but every unit I have worked with are decent human, I had no idea really what the forces were like, I just assumed they were all fighting men but I was so wrong, the modern army consists of DR's/nurses/engineers/chef's/I.T. specialist and many more professions, I would hate to think of the situation if they had followed government orders to confront the infected instead of taking a defensive stance.

Saturday 15th August

Today restored my faith in humanity and in particularity the humanity of the British people which nowadays only consists of English and welsh folk. Early this morning a group of around a hundred former protection officers from the community we had passed on our way here. They were directed to army HQ, the former council house and a few houses adjoining it. A crowd gathered outside and we were quite fearful of what they wanted. By mid-afternoon, an emergency meeting was called at the cathedral which is no longer a makeshift canteen but a building for multi-faithed people, our population here now is about four thousand people of all faiths/colour and gender, the army had installed a loudspeaker system for the people who could not get in. The meeting was called because the former protection officers had argued that they were the legitimate custodians of society and the army should relinquish the policing of the community to them. One of the senior protection took the pulpit and explained that the army was/is a temporary measure which was needed in times of emergency but now ST David's was secure it was time for the protection officers to return to power, this was met with many groans and surprisingly a few cheers from our community. No way was I having this, after listening to him for about half an hour, he foolishly opened the floor to questions, very bad move. I stood up and explained who I was and asked if they had the same policies as the former government, the dickhead replied yes to this and my blood boiled. I explained to him about the nursery we had found and the fact that the protection officers had locked the gates with living inside and summarily executed parents trying to get inside to their children, he had nothing to say except that it was deemed necessary at the time, I noticed several of his colleges put their heads down in shame. I also asked what their policy was to the Muslims/Jews/gays and travelers in our community, he stumbled a bit on this but gave the answer that suitable accommodation would be found for these outsides of the city and they would be well cared for, I was fucking fuming and asked if he was referring to relocation camps. This guy had no shame and explained that was exactly what he meant. There was uproar in the audience and many tears, the people surged towards the front and I thought that the crowd was going to lynch them, then a shot rang out fired by the leader of the army General Sir Peter Kenny. this quietened the audience and sir peter returned to the pulpit, he was calm invoice but you could see the anger in his face, he explained that the army was not here to take control but to help and if the people wanted the protection officers to return it was their choice. After several arguments mainly from the former protection officers, the choice was put to the people and anyone wishing for the return of the protection officers should raise their hands, about a dozen hands went up inside the cathedral and several in the crowd outside we were told, the next vote was for the army to carry on policing us and the show of hands were overwhelming. It was decided there and then that there was no room in our new society for hatred and bigotry and the protection officers should leave. Sir Kenny also stated that if required that the newly formed people's council should look towards establishing their own police force. This went down well but the leader of the council stood up and explained that at this time the majority of the people were quite happy with the army policing us, this bought a massive round of applause and Sir peter explained that the vote would also be put to the people in St Asaph/Anglesey/Usk//Buxton/Eyemouth and several other areas, plus it would be put before the king and the princes. I noticed the look on the protection officers face, the twats had no idea how organised the army was and how many communities they had saved. What was also a shock for me was that King Charles the 3rd and his family were safe, in hindsight I should have known that they would be the army's priority to save them. To be fair part of me was pissed off about this because I was not a royalist and saw the family as an over-privileged lot of tossers. I would not now voice these opinions but none the less, they remain mine. The meeting broke up and the former protection officers left the building to a round of jeers and quite a few thrown tomatoes, I had to laugh as some people knew the agenda of the meeting before coming here and had armed themselves appropriately.

Sunday 16th August

The army reckons two more days and ST David will be clear of the infected, it will be good to stop killing the dead, certain that two months ago that would have been classed as an oxymoron but times have changed a lot since then, we headed to the last few streets and saw that the barrier that the engineers erect after we have cleared an area was down and a couple of guys with lorries were actually releasing the dead from their trailers, I had no idea what was going on but it seems the army did, they soon dispatched the dead and approached one of the lorries only to be shot at by the driver and his mates, there was a small gun battle and obviously the army outnumbered them so it was over quite quickly, the other lorry started to drive away but suddenly a helicopter gunship appeared from nowhere and sprayed the road in front of it with bullets, the vehicle stopped and three guys got out with their arms in the air, the army approached them, there was a few raised words and they were put into a personnel carrier. I was too far away to hear what was exchanged so I went over to Jono and asked what the crack was, he explained that the three guys from the lorry and their dead friends were from the walled community of protection officers and trying to undermine the security of ST David's. They were to be taken to HQ to be questioned. There was nothing to do but carry on with our work and wait to find out why.   There were only two more streets to clear that day so Jono and a couple of others headed back with the prisoners. The rest of the day went well but I could not thinking our job was pointless if this kind of threat was to become the norm.

Monday 17th August

There is still massive amounts of work to do and most of it
has to be done by us with illness's because most Necessities
such as Pharmaceuticals and specialist hospital equipment
was either in hospitals or industrial estates bordering the big
cities but for now I am taking a much deserved two weeks
break mainly to get to know Jono a bit better and to get the
flat sorted. We heard today what happened with the troops
sent to sort out the mess with the protection officers,
apparently the dickheads started shooting as soon as our lot
turned up, luckily they were in armoured vehicles so no
causalities on our part, unfortunately or fortunately
depending on your views, the same cannot be said for them.
One of our vehicles crashed through their front gate and took
out a number of protection officers, after a small gunfight
they surrendered and our guys put the ultimatum to them,
out of a population of over 300, 47 people decided to pack
their belongings and join us, the remainder, mainly high
ranking protection officers and their families decided to stay,
their senior commander was arrested and returned with the
troops to face charges against humanity for his stupid little
stunt with the dead. I am certain that he will not receive the
death penalty, luckily the town of Usk is a thriving
community and they have a prison there.   I imagine that
elsewhere in the country there will be quite a few
communities made up of protection officers as they all lived
in walled estates because they would have been burnt out if

they lived with the general population. Hopefully their other communities are like this one and know absolutely nothing of each other's existence. I just hope this is the final nail in the coffin for them. There will be another meeting for the community this afternoon to discuss the new threat but Jono came over last night for something to eat and filled me in, it seems that the guys who had brought the dead here were seriously ill civilians from the protection officers camp who were ordered at gunpoint to deliver their cargo to our city to either wipe us out or to reduce our confidence in the army and welcome the protection officers back. I was not really shocked at this because prior to infection they had total control over society and must have hated the fact that society here was thriving without their rule.   I asked why the guys did not just dump their lorries outside the city and seek sanctuary here but it appears that they had family being held hostage back at their community. On a brighter note Jono stayed the night after explaining he was sick of bunking with his unit and asked if he could move in, this made me really happy for the first time in ages, I know a few weeks is not a long time to know someone but these days you took joy where ever you could find it, I actually cared for Jono a great deal, we had become firm friends and this just seemed the natural progression to our relationship. I obviously said yes to him and received the biggest hug I have had in years. We carried on with our work throughout the morning and by lunch we were certain that we had cleared ST David's. Woo Hoo!!! I have a lover and a friend rolled into one, even the protection officer's scheme could not wipe the smile off my face today. Jono and everyone else headed off to the meeting but I was shattered so went back to the flat I had taken over in the center of the city to sleep.

Tuesday 18th August

Had a good day today, Me and Jono took Max to view some of the deserted stores in town earlier to see if we could pick something up to make the flat a bit more homely, we found a few useful things and after taking them home we headed to the park so Max could have a good run, the city was awash with construction noise, the engineers were taking no chances on the dead continuing to just turn around at the flimsy barriers they had erected, inside the barriers they were busy building very substantial brick walls, they only needed to be around six foot but they were at least two feet thick, the rest of the communities were doing the same in their towns. ST David's and ST Asaphs were the only actually cities to be reclaimed from the infected and that was only because of the small populations they had.   These places were after all our permanent communities and our new homes. The time and effort needed for the walls was a small investment for our future security. To be fair this did make us feel a lot safer and with volunteers, there must have been well over a thousand people joining in the effort to secure our city. After a good walk with Jono and Max, we decided to head home but first Jono went off to talk to a few friends in his unit. I left him to it and carried on home to make us some dinner, after an hour or so Jono returned and explained that we had received a message from the Public Health England

(PHE) Centre of Infectious Disease Surveillance and Control in north London, there were over a hundred scientist and DR's stranded and running low on food, they were asking for an immediate evacuation. It was decided that several of the troop-carrying helicopters would head out there tomorrow, the compound where they are is very secure and has a landing pad on the roof, the operation would take only hours and may better our chances of eventually isolating the virus with a hope for a cure or at least immunity to the infection.

Wednesday 19th August

We decided that even though we had a few weeks grace to live rather than survive, that we would go and help with the walls today, We both realised yesterday that with time on our hands the thoughts and stresses over the last few weeks came back to haunt us. To be fair, I have had it pretty easy compared to others, I have not had to fight the infected for my life or kill loved ones to survive. I only really had to fend for myself and have not taken responsibility for any other person life. Around midday we saw five of the helicopters heading east towards London, word had got around what their mission was and you could see the hope in people's eyes as they flew overhead. We continued with our work and you would be surprised with the speed the walls were going up, around 7ish the helicopters returned but they were to land outside the city whilst the survivors were thoroughly checked for infection. I knew Jono was eager to find out the state of London because it is/was his home city, so I told him to head off to the secure area outside the city where the scientist was taken. Jono arrived home around two in the morning and it was obvious he had a few too many drinks, I knew him well enough not to bombard him with questions and I did not doubt in my mind that once sober he would tell me everything. I warmed up the food I made earlier and left him to it but I told him straight that if he needed to talk I would stay up all night with him if needed, I was not taken up on the offer but received an amazing hug from him before I headed to bed.

Thursday 20th August

Jono did come to bed around 5 am, it was now 10 am and there was no way I was going to wake him, he needed the sleep badly. He awoke around 6 pm and joined me in the living room, I had already prepared some stew so we sat down to eat, I didn't push it and let him tell me the news in his own time. After 10 minutes he started to tell me that London was truly gone and was to be avoided at all cost, I suspected as much because in the early days the army had a different policy and their orders were to confront and kill the infected. They had no idea at the time no barriers were safe, the sheer numbers of the dead made even their most sturdy barricade crumble like balsa wood if they could see living prey beyond. The noise attracted them to a much smaller degree, some would head towards noise but the majority ignored it. Jono went on to say that it was obvious to the helicopters pilots that some boroughs put up a fight but were overwhelmed, there was no evidence of people trying to evacuate, all major routes out the in and out the city were virtually free of vehicles, surprisingly enough, something else was picked up, ALL major green parks in the city were virtually empty of the dead, it seems our infected do not have any desire to leave concrete and tarmac unless necessary. This phenomenon was also noticed on the way back from London, it seems the infected are using the motorways as corridors and not venturing off as the rule. They were just roaming from one concrete skyline to another with no interest at to the fields and woods. The M25 was now dotted with infected groups ranging from a few hundred to several thousand, on the plus side, there were clear signs now of decay, so eventually these fuckers would rot away. I knew Jono he had a daughter living in Islington but until he mentioned her, I would not intrude. I had no idea how bad it got at the beginning because I stayed home with Max and only ventured out rarely, Jono was part of the outer London defenses and he had told me of the seemingly endless hordes of infected overwhelming the living. There was nowhere to run and the newly infected looked just like the living, from a bite to turning the timing varied greatly depending on how bad the wound was, people with multiple bites or just deep ones turned within minutes but minor bites and scratches could take hours. It was chaos with the living running with arms spread to their loved ones, only to be bitten by them. Like myself, most people lived in cities nowadays, I think the estimates were about 92% of the population were urban dwellers.

Friday 21st August

Some good news today, a convoy came from ST Asaphs earlier with main engineers, they were here to sort out communications and also to fix up a commercial radio station to keep people informed about what the situation was in our land and hopefully others. I left Jono and Max in the flat and went for a long walk, I now know my way blindfold through the city because after my door to door work of the previous weeks. This place is now crowded, the population is almost a third above the previous occupants, even when society was still going strong pre-apocalypse, I was not fond of too much company and avoided crowds like the plague, I don't think this will be my new forever life. I don't have to look to the future that much, I know they have said that treatments will be available eventually but to be fair I had crossed that shit out my mind when I have offered it weeks ago at my local surgery. I will stay awhile though, just to get them the necessities from the cities, I am not sure how they will make out in the long run, I suppose that with the infected showing sure signs of decay, the scientist state that their actual rate of decomposition was a lot slower than a normal corpse and they estimated that within three to four years they will be nothing more than sludge piles with bones. Society could make it and thanks to the army, almost the entire structure to rebuild is there for them.   I just hope they have a bit more sense now, our growth is important but I would hate to think the population for us was not in the 70 million range in a hundred years. I imagine history has a way of repeating itself but I honestly think that if these people just got past the neuroses that society forces us to accept like politics/racism/religions/ bigotry/mistrust and so on, that they could make a more balanced world. I have not even had a joint and I'm dreaming of a society where the water/electricity/phone and sewer workers get the praise and best pay, instead of the footballer/sports-personalities/reality TV stars/new readers/MP's and the health and safety execs. Nope, this society is not for me, I suppose I better talk to Jono. On the way back I bumped into Jillian, at first I did not recognise her, then she re-introduces herself as the record keeper from Nottingham castle. I happily shook her hand because I knew she would have info on the total population of all the communities combined. They are I suppose three types of survivors, us the ill, also the strong practical types who had escaped the cities and the people of the countryside whose lives have not changed except of course for All forms of social media being dead, including TV and radio. Jillian explained that I gave her some names when we met and after recently visiting St Asaph and leaving with their census of the surrounding countryside, she has discovered that my sister y and her partner and two of her four children were living in a village called Llannefydd. I suppose I am lucky, most people have no one left, as a rule, groups of survivors rarely escaped the city unless of course, they had many ill in their groups. I thanked Jillian and was genuinely happy, hey, who knows, we are a big family, maybe others got out in time. I will have to sort out suitable transport tomorrow and head to Llannefydd.

Saturday 22nd August

I invited Jono to come for the four hours' drive and he happily agreed, I had decided not to rush things and stay to help the communities to recover, this will not be long term but I am thinking a couple of years at least. I do not want to stay until I get ill and have no choice but to die somewhere I did not want to be. I have spoken to several DR'S back in st David's and a couple has assured me that if I choose not to receive treatment in the future that they would provide me with the name and amount of medication to take when needed for a painless end. I have become so fond of Jono but with my illness and his future frontline duties, a long term relationship was never planned. The Journey was pretty uneventful, There is nothing much here except industrial-scale farms and a few smaller holdings, there were a few villages we had to pass but this was as simple as stopping at their sturdy barriers and honk the horn, as I said earlier the country people have lived virtually under siege for many years, nothing on the scale of the mass pillaging after the food riots of five years ago, but they still suffered urbanites stealing their crops/live stocks. Both me and Jono were city dwellers and we were surprised/shocked at what we saw, we both assumed that fortified farms were futuristic things and well-armed but it seems that besides the industrial company farms that had high fences and razor wire around their outer fields, the smaller farms had given up half of their furthest fields to at least ten-foot-high thorn bushes surrounding their lands, I had no idea such a simple thing could work to keep out thieves. This, of course, would just as well for the infected, I smiled at this because I had still not given them a name except infected, I have referred to them as dead but even though I know they are, I still find it hard. The commonest term is biters but depends on what community you live in. We saw a group of 20 or so when joining the main road, we radioed the info but other than that the countryside is infection-free. We arrived at Llannefydd at about three o'clock and parked at their pub. The place was well kept and we went into the pub, Max was happy, he likes car rides but he is more interested in the exciting destination. He was in his element entering the pub, this meant a fuss and nibbles for him as a rule. Max was not disappointed, there was few in but Max made his way towards a group in the corner who had dared to mutter the word cute, I left him to it and headed to the bar, it seemed so normal, the barman even asked us what we wanted, the bar was well stocked and he explained they had lager on tap still, apparently there are a few working breweries a few miles away, not a brewery as in mass production but ample for locals. I was tempted but explained why I was here and who I was looking for, He knew Wendy and even told me my niece Keeley worked his bar at night. I thanked him and told Jono to enjoy a pint whilst I went to talk to Wendy. Max decided to come too, I knocked on the door and she answered, she just froze then gave me a massive hug, I was in bits, I'm not great at emotions at the best of time but this got to me, as far as we knew, we were all that is left of our family. Adam and Keeley joined us at the kitchen table, Nick, her partner was at his allotment getting some bits for tea. Wendy explained that being a nurse, she saw some of the first cases at the hospital and she saw one of her friends/colleagues turn into the infected, she knew straight away that things would get worse and decided there and then to head home and ring her kids to explain the situation, Keeley and Adam made it home but Chelsea and James lived in Leicester and by the time they had organised their stuff any travel was suspended and if you were found driving, you were either shot or detained. Wendy got some supplies in and also had the new solar panels that could run home, They stayed put for a couple of weeks whilst society went to pot, Keeley was the one who noticed that their neighbours with open curtains were attacked as soon as a person was visible to the infected. To be fair, they did not see much violence because they lived in a cul de sac and one of their neighbours had blocked the main entrance after the first houses were attacked. Luckily Nick had a very well paid engineering job and had purchased a new electric people carrier a few months earlier. After almost two weeks, their food was running short so they decided to head to nicks sister in wales. They were shocked that the roads were clear but explained that even with food running low, they were more scared of the protection officers stopping them than they were of the infected. She asked how I had survived and I explained the infected were not bothering me, she knew straight away what the crack was and asked what illness I had, St Asaph's had their radio station up and running for over a week now and all vital info about the infection was broadcasted to the people. After a few more tears, I explained I had to head back with Jono, Wendy asked if we would stay the night and join them for some tea later, and the pub had rooms so I headed to Jono and asked him what he wanted to do.

Sunday 23rd August

We did stay and had a nice chicken salad for tea, washed down with some amazing local cider. We could not get rooms though so the landlord offered us two blow-ups to bed down in the bar after closing, he explained that every room within 40 miles was full because of an influx of survivors. This morning just before we headed off, Wendy came up to us with a fully packed hamper, explaining that the village had more than enough to go around, I hugged Wendy tightly, I think we both realised that we may not see each other again but I did promise to try and visit again. Jono wanted to go to St Asaphs before heading back, to see what kind of set up they had. I left him to it and decided to take a look around. St Asaph's was nice but overpopulated, I wondered what would be done about this in the future, Wales except for the big cities was relatively free of the infected but with the influx of survivors the two small cities we had regained were just not enough to cater for the population, There was virtually nowhere in the surrounding countryside for them because the homes were already taken by the thriving communities that already lived there. I knew no-one here so I and Max headed to the park, I wish I had not after seeing a sizable crowd listening to a man explaining why he should be elected to the civilian council. He must have been a former protection officer as his views were solely based on the values of our former government, thank god he was booed and jeered after he explained that there were now many empty relocation camps and our surplus population particularly the Muslims/gays/Jews could be sent there. I headed back to the car to meet Jono after a couple of hours, there was no point in staying over because there just was not the room, on the way back Jono explained that he had spoken to several senior military men and the plan was to clear the islands around our coasts, once the islands were clear, there would be no need for walls and the surplus population could go there.

Monday 24th August

Pretty uneventful day, the army has assured us that by tomorrow we will have a working commercial radio station and we could pick up broadcasts from St Asaphs and Anglesey. I sat down with Jono after dinner and discussed the upcoming liberation of the islands. I was not sure if he would want to work in the same team as me because he might get some stick from others, he explained that he did not give a shit what others would say and explained that no one so far had given any of us crap and the old government policies were now firmly in the past, three protection officers had stood for election in ST Asaphs and not one of them gathered more than 40 votes, the future would be different, people were sick of the bigotry/intolerance and would not tolerate fascists in power anymore, I hoped he was right but I was scared that people do not change that quickly, even after the biggest disaster humans had faced. We had to keep the island plans hush-hush because it was going to be broadcasted on Saturday via the new radio system. King Charles was going to give a speech too.

Tuesday 25th August

Well, the army were true to their word, we now have the radio, it seems weird after the silence of the last few weeks but it will be nice to hear how we are doing as a whole. The first broadcasts were from ST Asaphs reporting on the current situation. The population under the protection of the army is now over a million and overcrowding has become an issue that will be addressed in the coming days. As far as England is concerned, there is no news at all from the south and military aircraft and satellite pictures have confirmed that there are some farming communities but nothing sizeable. The midlands are finished, there were just too many cities within a confined space and even the farms had given up and moved. There was the Buxton community and several in Yorkshire plus Northumberland, It was estimated that the entire population was lower than they thought and it stood at roughly between 2 -2.5 million, plus almost a million with serious ailments that make them immune. Several frigates had returned from the Middle East and were now patrolling the Irish Sea, there were a few ports that had been cleared of the infected on the coast and were now operational. Scotland had fared better than most and the country was scattered with communities, they were not happy that the British army had set up camp at eye-mouth but for now, they would accept it. After all, they were certain there was now no E.U. Oakham in Rutland had to be abandoned because they could not seal the town sufficiently and the 5000 or so survivors left had moved to ST Georges barracks at the former R.A.F Luffenham as a temporary measure but will have to be relocated. Many prisons are now refugee centres, there was no word what happened to the former inmates and I imagine most died in their cells of starvation after the staff left to take care of their families, the prisons are a good idea, they can hold a population of over 100,000 countrywide and most have high walls or fences, a few years ago it became mandatory that all hospitals/ prisons and schools had their independent energy supplies plus prisons had industrial-sized kitchen gardens to supply them with the basics. On the world news, it was confirmed that India and Pakistan are now nuclear wastelands.   America and China had a limited strike nuclear war concerning an incident at the DMZ in Korea and no news had been heard from either country excepts for a few naval vessels that were now heading to British waters after being invited. Canada was doing well still, even though their cities were now open morgues the people in the towns in the surrounding countryside manage to secure themselves against the hordes. Western Europe is as good as dead, there were just too many cities and large towns spread across the continent for survivors to flourish. New Zealand has not had one case of their dead rising so far. Moscow and St Petersburg were nuked by their own governments to stem the infection spreading plus destroying both governments in their civil war but it came too late and no news has come from them in weeks. Some Nordic states were still doing ok, the reports about the freezing conditions making the infection dormant were true and the infected were easily dispatched. Many Greek islands seem to be doing fine, the water being a natural barrier, once an infected enters the water they cease to function and effectively die for real. King Charles 3rd will address the nation on Saturday and outline the plans for the future.

Wednesday 26th August

So much for three weeks leave, Jono has had to return to ST Ashaphs to plan for the push into the islands, he will be there a week or so, I, on the other hand, was at a loose end, sure I had a few friends here most of them were in the army and were busy preparing for the future, I was asked several times what they were up to but no way was I going to break my word to Jono about their plans. It was a beautiful day so I decided to head with Max to White sands bay, it was only about two miles away and it had been cleared of infected well before St David's because in total there were only around 40 or so around. I manage to get a fresh loaf from the now working bakery and some ham, food was not a problem anymore, I expected to be eating tinned food for the foreseeable future but with all the farms nearby up and running I had not opened a tin of anything in days, we had fresh meat/fruit/veg/bread and butter, I got a couple of bottles of cider and some food for Max, plus of course some of my weed and set off. We reached the coast after about an hour and to my surprise there were several people there enjoying their day, I put my backpack down and stripped to my boxers as soon as we hit the sand, the sea looked amazing and this was the first time I had seen it in years, I headed straight in and so did Max, this surprised me because he was young and had never seen the sea before but he loved it. After a good swim we settled down for a bite to eat. after food I decided to spark a joint and open some cider, I chose a secluded area because people still had hang-ups about drugs but to my surprise, a young couple approached me and asked if I had any spare, I gave them an eighth from my backpack, I was not too fussed about the weed since meeting a local farmer David who ran a market garden/farm, he had fields of poly-tunnels growing all sorts of fruit and veg but kept one solely for marijuana. They invited me and Max to join them and some friends further down the beach for a cookout, I smiled at this because even though America was dead, their language had survived. I headed off with them down the beach to a group of twenty or so young people, I say young but late 20's early 30's was the norm. I felt a bit conspicuous because of my age but there were no worries on that score, I was made to feel very welcome. The only thing missing from their group was the lack of children, as a rule, children and the elderly did not survive the troubles in the cities, there were, of course, children in the countryside but they were kept well away from people just in case. The day turned to evening and I made my excuses and headed home but not before I gave the couple I met directions to David's farm. We were both shattered by the time we got back and I headed off to bed.

Thursday 27th August

It's weird how attached you become to someone, without Jono I felt lost as if part of me was missing, this pissed me off as I don't get too close to people as a rule because I hate getting hurt emotionally. It was late when we got up so I took Max straight out for a walk, we went over to the wall to see if any help was needed but there was no need, one of Jono's best friends Ian from the army came over and told me that they had so many volunteers that the work would be finished within days.   He suggested we meet up at the pub for lunch and catch up, to which I agreed to eagerly, he picked up on this and gave me some friendly ribbing about missing Jono and headed back to work but not before quietly reciting a small jingle about me and Jono sitting in a tree, the tosser made me smile at this. I headed towards the centre again to check the bulletin boards outside the council house, we were still under the protection of the army and they write the rules, don't get me wrong they were doing a great job and had outlawed discrimination of any form, their view was that we were all survivors and everyone was equal now. We did have a small group of 20 or so people who wanted to restore the ways of the last five years but they were firmly told that if they wanted to continue with their hate that they would be escorted to the protection officer's compound, I think this scared them and the bigots have kept their heads down. I met Ian as planned and we sat down to a ploughman's lunch and a pint of ice-cold cider. Ian was a good bloke and started off apologising about his mocking earlier and hoping I was not offended, I laughed at this and explained that I took his comments in good spirits. There was a lot of small talks then Ian opened up about how he sees' the future of our nation. He explained that almost every coastal town in Britain and many small inland towns, as well as 80% of the countryside, had green energy now after the blackouts of 2020, post-no-deal Brexit, he also explained that with the now diminished population foodstuffs would not be an issue for decades and then only if we overpopulate like before, his thinking was that if we can just survive the infected for three more years everything would be for the taking, at the minute, they had to rely on the million or so immune to go to cities to extract much-needed equipment. The most worrying problem at the minute is that the two small cities we have reclaimed cannot cope with the population we have and they desperately needed more space. Even after clearing Port Talbot they just cannot cope, He mentioned that plans were being made up and left it at that. We both knew each other knew those plans because he was Jono's bestie and I was his lover but we would not betray his confidence to the other.

Ian left after an hour to return to duties, he has set up home with a nurse not far from our place and invited me and Max to supper. I decided to stay for one more drink. Tomorrow I am going to volunteers to pick up some supplies they need from the cities, I can't sit around twiddling my fingers until Jono got back.

Friday 28th August

Had a lovely dinner at Ian and Sue's last night, they even mashed up an entire meal for Max, he loved it, certain he thinks he is human because he is not happy eating cold dog food as a rule. We heading to the army HQ to offer our services, was not even there five minutes before I were offered a job picking up medical supplies from a Pharmaceutical warehouse near Swansea docks. I was paired up with a guy called John because he could drive the new electric HGV's liberated from Port Talbot and I had my F.L.T license, he did not look too happy with Max but he was coming no matter what.   John was an absolute twat and I know after today that I will not work with him again, the entire journey there he gave me his views on what to do about overcrowding in our cities, with the prisons being reclaimed, they could send the Muslims and Jews there, I inwardly groaned but asked out of pure spite what we should do about the gays? We have many gay men in our communities, unfortunately, that is because many are HIV+ and were/are immune to the infected, Johns plan it seems would be to get the usage out of the queers as in reclaiming goods from cities and then send them to the prisons without their meds to let them die. I was not about to out myself to this wanker but I had to ask why he was immune, he mistook my question and explained he was not a poof and has respectable cancer. I had heard enough so I shoved my earphones in. I know I should have defended others and myself but to be fair, this ignorant twat did not warrant my time or anger. We got to Swansea within hours and found the warehouse, it was in a high-security industrial I area totally fenced off, and we unlocked the gate and secured it afterwards as the inside had been cleared by previous forages. John backed up to the loading bay and I got out, expecting John to do the same but he just sat there and smiled, I asked if he was coming in and he replied that his job was to drive, the work ahead was mine and would I wake him when I finished. As I said tosser. I noticed the next warehouse down was a well-known personal electric vehicle specialist, thing such as electric mopeds and scooters, I knew the city was a few miles away and I figured John would not be into a detour there so I unpacked a new electric moped and plugged it in, this being a port I knew it ran on green energy from the wind farms. The work was not difficult as all I needed was written down, I did not understand half the words but the crates were labelled so I just matched the word, it took several hours to fill the HGV and I was starving, I did not bother to ask john to accompany me and headed to the city on the now charged moped. John must have been awake and shouted after me but I just shouted I would be back in a couple of hours, Max loved sitting on the wide footrest panel and I did not go too fast, as we entered the city everything seemed so calm again, I remember experiencing this in derby, There were infected about but very few and showing signs of deterioration. The thought struck me again that most people had died in their homes probably of starvation or thirst because they were too scared to leave, imagine a place where the civilian protection officers or any police force were more terrifying than the walking dead. I walked around for a while until I found what I was looking for, I had to break the window to get through the door to the computer/ phone shop, I know it's an odd thing to do for but my mission was to get as many 128gb up to a 1tb USB sticks and micro SD cards as possible. They were for David the farmer, CD's/DVD' had gone the way of the dinosaurs in the last few years and digital files is where it was at, David had a massive database of films/music and porn on his laptops and wanted to back up everything plus give gifts to friends. He is a tech-head at heart and feels that one day the net will return. They were three reasons I was doing this, firstly and most importantly, I could exchange these for fresh veg/fruit and more importantly, weed. Secondly, I believed him about the net, and thirdly, I like the guy.   After I had finished I popped into a supermarket nearby, the door was wide open and several real dead bodies but here there were signs of looting, I made my way to the frozen section and the freezers were still full, I knew they would be working but I expected no food. I reclaimed a part of microwave chips and kebabs plus food for max. I made my way into the back of the store looking for a break room with hopefully a microwave. I found what I was looking for and sat down to eat, there were

security camera screens in the next room fully working and I
went to check them. they had stopped recording on the 21st
of last month so I rewound one of the film files to a few days
prior until I saw activity on the screen, The protection officers
had pulled up in four lorries on the 18th July and ordered
several Asian survivors at gunpoint into the store to loot for
them, I assumed the people sent in were immune until I
witness one of them being eaten alive by the infected in the
store. I had seen enough and turned it off. We headed back
to the moped and set off for the docks, John was fuming with
me and asked what the fuck was so important, sometimes I
can be a bitch and replied: "to spend less time with you".
Needless to say, not a word was spoken on the way back. As
soon as we parked at the main industrial estate in ST David's
I jumped out and headed to HQ without a word to john. I
took another job for tomorrow afternoon, this one was
pretty easy though, I just had to take a van to USK filled with
equipment for them to start up their radio system. Before
leaving the headquarters I explained that I would not be
working with John again, this was met with smiles from him
and a colleague, they apologised and explained they normally
send him out alone on small jobs because he is a dick and
that Johns views are well known and he has been spoken to
about it but they fully accept my decision.

Saturday 29th August

I headed out early to Usk because I wanted to be back in

range to listen to the kings' speech at 3 pm, I reached the town by 10.30 but as soon as I saw the barricade down I realised that something was very wrong, they had not had the chance to build walls as of yet so they had used shipping containers to ward off the infected, this was a really good idea as a rule but somebody had used a JCB to remove them from several streets, the dead were everywhere and I am talking thousands of them. I had never seen such a concentration of them like this is the countryside before now. I left the track by the barricades and headed in on foot, there were bodies everywhere, I am guessing that whatever happened occurred during the day because most were dressed in shorts or floral dresses. I walked the entire distance of the town to the barricades on the other side only to witness hundreds of bodies with bullet holes, mostly really dead but several walking, it seems the town folks had rushed here hoping to escape into the countryside but were met by shooters, I could and would not believe that the army was responsible for this. I headed back through town and as I passed the prison several voices shouted out to me from behind the gate, I approached them and spoke to a couple of army guys through the bars, it seems that a large group of protection officers from a community in Chepstow had approached these people several times offering protection and to deal with their undesirables by placing them in a relocation camp a few miles away. This was flatly refused by the people here so the protection officers had lured around ten thousand infected from the motorways to Usk, it would have been pretty easy to do because all you needed was one living person in view on a vehicle and the infected would follow forever. The townspeople who fled headed straight into an ambush by the protection officers who opened fire on them. I asked how many were in the prison and was informed about 400, I was shocked, 400 out of a population of 5000, this was nothing short of genocide. I explained who I was and that I would head straight back to St David's and get help to them A.S.A.P. I headed back to the truck and set off home, I got back a lot quicker than I thought, I must have been hitting 70mph without realising it and scolded myself, I have survived the end of the world and did not want to die in a crash. I headed straight to HQ and spoke to a senior officer about what I had discovered in Usk. He quickly made several radio transmission and thanked me before heading off to transmit the news to Anglesey and St Asaph. I headed to the pub with Max, god knows I needed a drink after today, I was only there for five minutes before someone came and asked if it was true about Usk, the news gets around really fast in small communities like ours. I waited until everyone had quietened down before addressing the room, I explained everything I knew about the situation in Usk and did not spare the details, there was total silence when I finished except for John who I had worked with yesterday on the Swansea run, he was sat on his own in the corner and declared loudly that Usk was full of sexual deviants and followers of false gods, they deserved their fate and the protection officers were right to rid the country of scum. I imagine there was not one person in the room who did not want to lynch the bastard and their protests grew louder, several confronted John but he was set in his ways, there was going to be trouble so I pushed passed the crowd around John and to my utter shame I threw a punch and knocked him clean out, there were several cheers to this but I felt nothing but shame for my actions and headed home to get stoned.

Sunday 30th August

I missed the Kings speech Yesterday, I just got wrecked because of my shameful actions towards John. Part of me was expecting to be arrested for assault so I headed to the HQ to see if I was in bother, on my way I received several slaps on my back and plenty of smiles, I knew John was not popular but I still felt shame. After arriving at the HQ, I asked if John had made an official complaint and was informed that yesterday afternoon John and several others had left our community to join the protection officers at Chepstow. The army had already sent troops to Usk and once the survivors were safe they would deal with the protection officers once and for all. They knew of several camps that were in their charge and intended to deal with all of them, the officer explained that the army is trying to restart society and they cannot have the protection officers undermining them. I left them to their plans and headed to the pub, this time though I was not after a drink, I knew I could get all the info on yesterday's speech and any plans the army has. The speech went down well by all accounts, king Charles spoke candidly about our future and what it would entail, The immediate plan was to head to the isle of man to clear the infected and once successful they would move on to the channel islands. It was mentioned that a new interim government had been set up and it was now law that discrimination of any form will NOT be tolerated, the new United Kingdom would be a multicultural/multiracial society, there was even talk of inviting Scotland to rejoin the union once they have stabilised. A scientist was stating that after trying to inject troops with curable illness's for the infected to ignore them had failed in every test. It was vital for the reclaiming of the islands for any immune to volunteer immediately for service, It was decided that initially, ferries would take the armoured vehicle over and they would clear the port of Douglas and then ten thousand armies/naval and air force troops would be shipped over, plus as many immune as possible. The pub was buzzing with the news and I had never been to Manx so I was excited also. I know the population of immune was roughly a million but we had people with illness's coming in daily since most cities were bombarded from the air with flyers stating who we were and our location. I immediately headed to HQ to offer my services, as soon as I got there the queue of hundreds was waiting to get in to offer their services, this made me feel immensely proud. I queued as is the British way and waited my turn, it seems that the plans for the islands was well underway and the first ferries would set out today and hopefully followed by the main force within days, this worried me because I wanted to hopefully work with Jono's unit again but I might not see him in time. I headed over to Ian Jono's friend to discuss it with him, He is a really good guy as I said earlier and after I had shared my concerns, he bought a list out of volunteers who would be working with their unit, he apologised for jumping the gun but there at the top of the list was my name, I could have hugged him there and then but instead thanked him, I stayed for tea with him and Sue and then a few drinks, Sue must have scented my weed because she asked very sternly if I had any on me, I thought she was going to lecture me until she smiled and explained that our new community was about sharing and I should build a joint. Even Ian tried some but he was not used to it and fell asleep, Sue it seemed was very used to it and we ended up smoking an eighth between us, before leaving about 1 am I gave her the location of Dave's farm and explained he had good stuff.

Monday 31st August

I got home around 2ish in the morning because it was a muggy night and I decided to walk with Max, upon arriving home, I was met with the words "you dirty stop out". I was never so happy to see another human being and gave Jono another of my big soppy hugs. We filled each other in on what the last few days had given us, he knew about Usk of course and I had never seen him so angry, he explained that a meeting of senior officers and the king had decided enough was enough and all known protection officers compounds were to be offered the chance to join us or to be destroyed, Chepstow was a different matter altogether, the civilians would be made the offer but all protection officers there would be arrested and charged with crimes against humanity, he went on to say we could not live like this anymore. Their way was history now and the sooner they accepted that, the better. We also discussed the upcoming invasion of the Islands, this cheered him up and he explained that once the islands had been cleared things would become much better and people could live as opposed to surviving. I explained I had tea with Ian and Sue and that Ian had already put my name to their unit's volunteers, I also told him about Ian's little song about us sitting in a tree k.i.s.s.i.n.g. This put Jono in a good mood as he explained the tosser would get a slap around his head as soon as he sees him. We left it at that and went to bed. We did not wake until around 11 o'clock and Jono was miffed because he had so much organising to do. I left him to head to his unit and arranged to meet him later in the pub, I know I keep mentioning the pub but I'm not a heavy drinker, it is just that it was our local and everything you needed to know was discussed there, plus it was cozy. I went about my business as we had only days left before we set off to Douglas on the Isle of Man, I am certain we will be their weeks because the population is around 90 thousand plus the former government and their flunkies. I was thinking of leaving Max with Sue but to be honest to myself I knew he would come along. I went shopping for some things for supper, I splashed out on some steaks that I had swapped for liberated cigarettes from Swansea, there was an informal bartering system at the shops but even if you had nothing to barter you still got your food.   I met Jono and Ian at the pub around five in the evening and I got a friendly slap from Ian calling me a grass for telling Jono about his little song, we all laughed at this and settled down for a drink, Sue joined us after a hour or so and we invited them over for tea, I had got enough steaks to go around and with fresh new potatoes and salad, it should be a nice meal. We headed back to the flat and after eating Jono explained that he and Ian had a lot of planning to do, I suggested to Sue that we could grab a couple of the communal bikes and head over to David the farmer I had a mention, she smiled at this and readily agreed. Max wanted to come too but I could not let him run the whole way so decided to leave him, the little sod knew the eyes would not work on me so he gave them to sue, this worked a treat for Max as Sue explained that she has seen one of those baby-carrying bike trailers at one of the stores in town. I smiled inwardly at Max, he was happy as Larry that he was coming. We got the trailer and fixed it to one of the bikes and set off to David's, it was only three miles away and we made it in no time. David's was pleased to see us and even happier when I gave him about 30 1tb USB sticks and double that in SD cards, he thanked me and explained we could have as much as we could carry, I told sue to get some as I would not be needing any until after the invasion of the islands, I do like my weed but no way was I putting non-immune in danger, my job would be clearing houses again and I needed to have my wits about me. After sharing a cider with David we made our excuses and headed for home but not before David came and gave us both a massive hug, he whispered in my ear to be careful and come back safe, I told you he was a nice guy and I happily gave him a tighter squeeze and explained I would be back in a few weeks for some weed.

Tuesday 1st September

The Army units that went to Usk with at least 100 immunes decided to save the town as all the barricades were up except for the place where the dead were shepherded in, they used the same technique to rid the town of the majority by driving a flatbed truck around with two terrified soldiers on the back shouting at the dead before leading them away. The soldiers went street to street killing what was left and of course, the immune went door to door, it would take a few days before they could be sure it was clear but with overcrowding elsewhere, the effort would be worth it. During the day several units were dispatched to the known protection officers camps but Chepstow was a different matter, thee helicopter gunships were sent with ground troops. We heard reports by early evening that only one camp fully surrendered and offered allegiance to the new government, the other three including Chepstow put up a hell of a fight, obviously they were outnumbered and outgunned and the fight did not last long. Only four surviving officers from Chepstow were arrested and the population of around 300 seemed greatly relieved to be rid of their brutal overseers. In the end, all their communities were left intact because after the protection officers were either killed or arrested, the civilian population greeted our troops with open arms, most had no idea that society was being reformed in wales by the army and only stayed because of the security of their camps.

Wednesday 2nd September

The town was buzzing today, everyone was excited at the upcoming invasion and it's positive implications for our future. Several units were loading Lorries at the HQ and the immune had commandeered a vast variety of vehicles to head to Anglesey for the ferry journey, I thought we had a few days but it seems that we will be getting the ferry at 3 am to get to Douglas by early light. There was no time for goodbyes and I went to find Jono's unit. We set out around 4 pm to Anglesey and our spirits were pretty high, apart from the first useless fight against the infected in the early days of the disaster, this was the first real push against the bastards, it would be tough because even with the military and immune, we were still outnumbered 3-1. When we arrived in Douglas the port was fully cleared and several shipping containers blocked the port from the mainland, from the ferry you could see the area beyond the barricades was awash with infected numbering in their thousands. It would be difficult to clear the town but once done we could use it as our staging ground to clear the rest of the isle. Just as we docked several jets flew over and dropped their payload on the masses of infected, they were using incendiary bombs which are very effective, after the bombs had been dropped and after the fires of funeral pyres had diminished several helicopter gunships set to on the still walking infected. The army was pulling out all the stops to make this mission a success. By midday the call was given for the army to move in and start their street to street searches, the pattern was that once an area had been cleared the engineers who had built effective moveable barriers moved in to secure the area, then we started again

Thursday 3rd September

Yesterday went well and we managed to clear a decent area of the town from the infected. The helicopters and planes are a godsend, they have been flying over the isle destroying all large concentrations of the infected, this just left us mopping up the smaller groups and individuals. Killing them permanently was not a big deal now as they resembled human beings less and less as they deteriorated. I still find it incredible that people chose to die at home rather than make a run for it. I suppose that by the time people did venture outside despite the risk from the protection officers they were too weak to ward off the infected. It was still tiring work and the makeshift tented city at the port was not the most comfortable, on the plus side the royal logistical corps served up meals to die for. I was trying to think what was different about this work compared to the clearing of ST David's then it hit me, Most people that we found in their homes were not victims of hunger or thirst, they were shot. It is looking like the protection officers had decided to kill the previous inhabitants rather than protect them. This surprised me because I assumed the government came ashore under the protection of the navy, I went to find Jono to ask what happened on HMS Queen Elizabeth. Jono was in the mess and I asked to talk to him in private, we went outside and I immediately asked if the high rate of murders in people's homes had anything to do with the military. Jono was silent for a minute and I thought the worst until he explained that within days of the government and their protection officers boarding the aircraft carrier there was an argument over who was in charge, the protection officers even though outnumbered had tried to arrest the senior officers on the ship at gunpoint this did not go down well and after several gunfights, the government was rounded up with the surviving protection officers and put ashore in Douglas, at the time Douglas was free of infection and deemed safe, within days of this happening several boats had made their way to the isle and brought the infection with them, the government had radioed the carrier asking for immediate evacuation but this was denied by the navy on board. I was glad I was wrong about the military being involved with the murders. This did make me wonder though, would it be classed as the shortest civil war in history? It did not matter because we all know the victors write history and I am certain none of these facts would ever be made public.

Friday 4th September

Was not looking forward to today, not that I look forward to any day dispatching the infected but last night everybody was talking about the amount of murdered people and it was harrowing seeing entire families slaughtered in the safety of their homes. We just had to put it behind us and deal with the job in hand. After a few hours of hard graft I heard shouting outside, I figured someone may need help so I ran out into the street to find out what was happening. A unit a few streets away had found ten survivors including three protection officers holed up in a former hotel, they survived because one of the survivors was seriously ill and had made daily forages to the surrounding homes for food. I went over to see for myself and join in the celebrations of finding living after almost two months. As I arrived there was an argument, the army wanted to arrest the protection officers straight away because it was certain that they had systematically murdered hundreds if not thousands of people. The argument was started by the survivors insisting that these officers had saved their lives. The army was unsure exactly what to do so shipped them all of to the port to be questioned by senior staff. We all went back to our work but with a much lighter heart if one group of survivors existed maybe others do too. We worked into the early evening but all we discovered were either infected or murdered people in their homes, I imagine that the protection officers were running low on ammo because the last hundred or so houses that we searched contained people with their throats cut as opposed to being shot. When we got back to the port for a much-needed rest the rumours were rife about the carnage the protection officers had committed. The two protection officers were separated from the survivors and placed in a now disued police station which was guarded with armed army personal for their security.

Saturday 5th September

We got up early to start our work today but during breakfast, a senior officer came in with news of the survivors yesterday. He explained that he would be attending all the breakfast sittings during the morning to repeat his factual news and to stem the rumours. According to the survivors, once the former government and the protection officers arrived things were fine for a couple of days until several infected had been noticed at the port and in the town, this caused panic and the townsfolk were told to go home and the protection officers would inform them when it was all clear. After a short gun battle the protection officers started going door to door, people assumed it was to tell them of the situation but word soon got around that they were killing healthy people to limit the amount of future infected. Once this was known, it seems the entire town fled their homes and in the chaos, the infection spread rapidly. As for the survivors of yesterday, they were saved by the protection officers with them to the point where they killed some of their ranks to defend the group. It seems that there is a compound further inland where members of the former Government and protection officers still exist. I was shocked because I heard the former government were either dead or infected. We were told that we should continue with our clearing work and that several units including air support had been sent to deal with them. There was nothing else to do except carry on and await some news.

Sunday 6th September

It was decided that today was going to be a rest day, in only three days we had cleared at least a third of the town and today was about luring as many infected as we could towards the port, this was a job for only a handful of people as I explained earlier in this diary. Jono and Ian asked if I wanted to go sailing with them, I thought it a bit odd but we all deal with things differently I suppose. There were many small sailing boats in the marina so I left them to find one and headed to the canteen to see if I could scrounge the makings of a cold lunch. I knew one of the chefs quite well after sharing a few joints with him in St David's, he was more than happy to supply me with what amounted to a be all the ingredients of a lunch worthy of any restaurants, normally I am a good cook and enjoyed preparing meals but I knew Ian would not let me near the galley on the boat because he loved cooking. I was not sure about sailing and assumed I would probably get seasick but I was wrong. Once we set off into the Irish Sea it was amazing, I had no idea you could get a rush from sailing, it was exhilarating speeding through the waves at what seemed an amazing pace. After a few hours we headed towards the coast and anchored in the calm water to have some lunch, Ian had whipped up a scrumptious meal and also found a bottle of wine in the main cabin, it was as if the whole apocalypse had never happened, certainly one of the best days so far. We rested for a while just taking in the peace of it all. By late afternoon we set sail back to the port, on the way back Ian came on deck smiling and apologised to us both for ruining our romantic afternoon. This made us both smile and I told him to be careful or I'd steal Sue off him and make her my official fag hag. We arrived back at the port around four o'clock and even though I thought nothing could shock or surprise me anymore, the sight of our former Prime minister and most of his cabinet along with around fifty protection officers with hands zip-tied behind their backs being frog marched onto a frigate beats everything. We all laughed when Mr Farage the minister for justice started shouting that the guards surrounding his group would all face a court-martial.

Monday 7th September

Back to clearing the houses today but even though the work was morbid I had a spring in my step after yesterday's arrests. The three decent protection officers who had aided the survivors gave the army directions to the compound where the former government was holed up. The army did not give this lot any ultimatums this time, they rammed the gated entrance to the compound and after being fired at they killed several protection officers and the rest of the community surrendered. The former ministers and protection officers were arrested and bound. We found no more survivors the rest of the day but reports were coming in that possibly thousands had been murdered in their homes, I cannot imagine the sheer terror they must have felt at the hands of the protection officers. We worked well into the evening today because we wanted the town cleared as soon as possible, knowing that once we had secured the isle we would head back to the mainland and let the next batch of soldiers/immune head to jersey whilst we rested before being sent to Guernsey. There was talk of eventually moving on to clear Ireland but this was quashed by senior army personal stating that Northern Ireland was no longer a British province and besides the fact we would not be welcomed by possible survivors, it was not the remit of the army to offer assistance to a foreign power until we solved our problems.

Tuesday 8th September

We have now almost secured the entire town of Douglas, with over ten thousand troops plus the immune we should have the isle cleared within the week, unlike the mainland, there were plenty of infected in the countryside here as they had not had to fortify their farms and villages against hungry hordes from the city after the food riots of 2021. In some strange way, the crisis's after the no-deal Brexit was a godsend for many survivors who either lived in the countryside or were residents of the relocation camps as they were safe behind barriers. Only the bravest and the immune escaped the cities rather than sit at home waiting for death to knock their door. Tonight there is a treat on at the docks to boost morale, they are showing a flick at an improvised outdoor cinema for the troops, I just hope they don't have a sick sense of humour and show a George A. Romero film. One other thing we can be thankful for is that like all coastal towns on the mainland, the islands all had green energy supplied by offshore wind farms. I am not going to watch the film though because I am going to spend a bit of quality time with Jono later at a reclaimed flat we have commandeered overlooking the sea. I have seen him constantly because we work the same unit but we don't rub our relationship in people faces and keep it professional, in fact except for a few close friends, not many people know we are lovers, it's not that we are hiding anything but neither of us is what you would call effeminate so we just let people assume we are friends. I know for certain that if anyone asked Jono about our relationship, he would happily tell them we are a couple.

Wednesday 9th September

Well so much for a romantic evening, Jono invited Ian around because the work was effecting him pretty badly and he is also missing Sue, to be fair I did not mind at all as Ian is a decent bloke, we had a nice evening chatting about the possible future of our communities, we all agreed that once the islands were clear that society could start to rebuild, we have the two cities and most of the countryside in wales but always with the threat that one day the hordes could overrun us. Our job here will be over here in a few days and once finished we will head back to St David's for some much-needed R&R. I for one am looking forward to it because I seem to be tired all the time these days, I think when I do get home I will have to go see a DR about how my illness is going.

Thursday 10th September

The town of Douglas is now clear of infected but to be certain of this we will go house to house once more whilst the army units and a few immune join the rest in the countryside, It is tedious work checking every nook and cranny where a human could hide but in the end, it will be worth the hassle. We heard the news from Anglesey earlier that the former Prime Minister had taken his own life rather than face judgment in court. The rest of the former cabinet and the protection officers are now securely locked up in Usk Prison awaiting trial, I imagine they will be there quite some time because we have much more important issues to deal with for the time being. The overcrowding in the mainland communities is now a number one priority and they are expecting to ship over 20,000 in the next week or so to ease the situation, it appears that even though there are no fortified farms here, the infected still preferred to remain in the towns and the countryside id relatively free of the infected. Most villages did not survive though because people fleeing Douglas took the infection with them. One exception to the rule is Foxdale, a village of around 700 people, they had the foresight to isolate themselves and fortify their community. It was a morale booster to hear of so many survivors but I could not help wondering how many surviving groups are out there in the world thinking they are alone.

Friday 11th September

We are pretty much certain now that Douglas is good to go, over 2,000 of immune have searched everywhere possible but we found no more infected. If all goes well, we will be heading home tomorrow. A few engineering units of the army quite a few immune will stay on to sort out a freshwater supply but other than that Douglas is ready for people to inhabit, once again, thank god for wind farms as the electricity on the islands has always been up and running. It's a bit creepy walking around at night with all the street lights on but no people around, one of our jobs going house to house was to switch off the electricity to the homes so at least they remained dark and less daunting. This is our units last night here and we are going to celebrate at a local pub this evening, I'm a bit miffed that I left my weed on the mainland because even though I enjoy a drink as a rule I do not enjoy getting drunk. The evening went well in the pub with everyone in high spirits about going home to ST David's tomorrow, one of the young soldiers in Jono's group had a bit of a pop at me regarding my sexuality, to me, it was water off ducks back because I had heard it all before but Jono took umbrage at this and walked over to me and gave me a passionate kiss then explained to the group that if anyone had any issues with it, they could come outside and try their hand at queer-bashing verbally or otherwise, there were a few shocked expressions from the younger soldiers but the majority of them smiled as they were veterans in their 30's who were taught in school that diversity in life was a good thing. The younger soldier who tried to belittle me looked very embarrassed and after explaining that he has had a few too many drinks apologised. I fully accepted his apology and told him there were no hard feelings. He did get a few telling off from his colleagues during the rest of the evening but other than that we all celebrated our accomplishments over the last few days.

Saturday 12th September

We were supposed to ferry back to the mainland today but during the night a fierce storm started up and it was decided to wait it out. The storm was one of the worst I had seen in years, the wind was well over 100mph and the rain was horrendous, it made me realise that summer was truly over now and we had months of winter to look forward to. The

stormed had cleared by early evening but it was decided that
we would not set off to the mainland until the morning. The
storm made me think about not just our future but the future
of the planet, like the human race, this would be a fresh start
for it too, you could see it in the countryside that there was
an abundance of wildlife flourishing without our
interference. This was a new beginning for the land too, no
more intensive farming to destroy the soil and the planet
would have time to heal, I was not sure of the entire world
population but I imagine it would number in the low
hundreds of millions as opposed to almost   10 billion
pre-apocalypse. I know I will not live to see society hopefully
grow into something different to what we had but to know I
was here when the seeds to that society were planted makes
me feel nothing but joy, this really is a new start for human
beings and even though I am an atheist I pray with all my
heart that we do not fuck it up again.

Sunday 13h September

Home, at last, it seems odd calling this flat in a strange city
home but with Jono that is what it has become. Max is happy
to be here too, as soon as we got in he went straight to his
bed to sleep, I think the excitement has been too much for
the poor little man. The weather is shit today so I think we
will just lounge around for the afternoon before heading out
to Ian and Sues for supper, There is one thing I have to do
though and that is to head to the Dr to get some blood work

done. I was not looking forward to this because I know in my heart that my illness has progressed. I headed off to the clinic whilst Jono and Max took a much-needed rest, As soon as I entered I was met with a big hug from Sue, after catching up I explained why I was here and she immediately showed me into the Dr, after taking some blood and examining me he gave me an appointment to come back in four days. There was nothing else for me to do but wait so I headed back to the flat to have a spliff and a JD and coke. Around 5ish we all headed over to Ian and Sues for some food and good company, I asked Sue not to mention my visit today until I was sure that it was my illness making me tired rather than just general fatigue. The evening went well and we filled Sue in on our adventures in the Isle of Man, she could not stop laughing at Jono's response to the tiny bit of homophobia I suffered on the last night in the pub over there.

Monday 14th September

The ferries set off today to the isle of Wight, the population there is roughly 140,000 so it would take a little longer than the clearance of the isle of man but I am sure that now we have the strategy of luring out the infected that it will not take too long. I thought we had at least a week together but Jono was called to HQ today, there has been trouble at the Buxton community, those fucking protection officers again, at least this lot have not lured the infected there but they are trying to enforce their rules on the people, Buxton was formed without the protection of the army, they just effectively blocked their town off from the infected and were doing well until senior protection officers turned up. They have asked for help over the communication system the engineers set up for them a few weeks ago. Jono's unit was to set off tomorrow to try and sort it out. I decided not to go along because I had no idea how long it would take and I had to find out my blood results in a few days, the rest of the day we spent just enjoying the peace and each other's company.

Tuesday 15th September

Jono's unit headed off first thing this morning and to be fair I was a bit jealous because Derbyshire is my home county and part of me would love to see it again. I was at a loss with what to do for the next few days, not only waiting for Jono to return but worrying about my results. I decided to grab one of the now abundant electric cars that the immune had commandeered from the dealerships in the cities and head over to Swansea to grab some electronic goods and data storage to exchange for some weed from Dave the farmer. I was surprised to find that several electric motor homes had been acquired from somewhere. I went to check to see if they were fully charged and chose a smaller one for me and Max. Electric Vehicles were now a communal property in our communities so we set off for Swansea. I had to stop at the main barricade to join the main road out of St David's but this was nothing more than a formality, the army had no problems with people leaving but anyone entering was thoughtfully examined for bites or scratches, not that anyone in their right mind would try to enter under those circumstances. I decided on the way that we would stay overnight in Swansea and make a little break for ourselves, Max loved the vehicle, he could either sit upfront with me or take a nap on the bed in the back. We arrived in Swansea without seeing any infected at all until we reached the new ring road but when we did the sight and smell was horrendous. There must have been tens of thousands of them just wandering along. I stopped the vehicle and just watched in amazement as the passed by twenty feet away without paying us any intention whatsoever. I said earlier that the wildlife was booming in the countryside but it appears that this was true for the cities too, there was a massive murder of crows following the infected swooping down on them to pick off what I assumed was maggots but they were tearing away at the loose flesh, I did not see that rats scurrying around their feet at first but after noticing them I almost gagged, they were eating them as they walked, I saw several with just bare-bones up to their knees. Thank god this infection had not crossed species as I know for certain that we could not fight flesh-eating rats or birds. After an hour or so the main horde had passed and only a few stragglers remained. I got out the marked maps that I got from the main foraging groups for this area, there were a couple of industrial estates not far from here so I headed to the nearest one. I found what I was looking for straight away, there was a curry's store right next to a Tesco, I could get the electronics and then grab some lunch. The curry store was locked up tight and it took a hour to break in but it was well worth it, I got a few hundred TB USB drives and twice as many micro SD cards with the same storage, I also took around 20 of the latest laptops, there was no internet of course but with the electricity we have, the laptops would be brilliant for watching films or listening to music and I knew Dave had petabytes of both. I would be able to get weed from him well into next year for this lot. After I had put all the stuff into the camper we headed to Tesco next door, this was not locked and people had been here but it was all intact, the smell from rotting fruit and veg was disgusting but the shelves were full as were the freezers. I grabbed Max some of the quality dog food plus some tinned hot dogs that he loved then I went looking in the freezers for a decent ready meal, I thank the universe once again for wind power and headed back to curry's to fire up a microwave. I was tempted to get a bottle of JD but I did not fancy getting sloshed. I decided I would come back here before heading home and grabbing some spirits though because I could barter them in ST David's. After a nice lunch for us both we headed into the city proper, there was no need to go there but I was just curious. I parked upright in the center of the city and headed off for a walk, I know that sounds odd but there was nothing to fear here for me except maybe desperate survivors but to be honest if there were survivors here they had everything for the taking, I did take a handgun though just in case. The streets here were teeming with infected and the smell was just as bad as the ring road, I saw a multi-story car park and decided to get an elevated view of my surroundings. From up here the city just looked like it was a Sunday morning, everything was intact and the only thing missing was living people, I got quite melancholy about what we had lost be also realizing that society and the planet needed this break. The world we had lost was at its closest to a nuclear war as it had ever been. I have described the situation in England but the global situation was much worse, many Middle East countries were at war with each other not over oil but clean drinking water. Refugees were counting in their tens of millions of invading countries just for the requirements of staying alive, those countries in return committed atrocities against them just to survive themselves. Western societies thought they were immune but climate change had affected them badly and most had food shortages, the fact was that 10 billion people was just too many for the planet to support. I decided to make a joint and just chill up here for a while, Max was content, he had fed well and I had a two-liter bottle of water with us. I just sparked up my spiff and was looking down at the infected passing when a young bloke appeared on a bike with a trailer on like the one I used for Max. Not infected and immune so I shouted down to him, the guy fell off his bike in fright at my voice so I waited until he got sorted then shouted again, he looked up at me and gave me the biggest grin I have ever seen, after a few shouts back and forth and my assurance I was not a protection officer I told him I was coming down. As I approached him he looked nervous so I told Max to go and say hello first, Max ran straight to him and after sniffing him thoroughly started making a fuss, I knew Max well and I had seen him turn his nose up and head back to me with dodgy people so I smiled and introduced myself, His name was Stephen and I was the first person he had seen in over six weeks, I asked why he had not headed up to one of our communities because even now I could see the flyers scattered around that the helicopter had dropped a few weeks ago, he said he had no idea anyone had survived as he had only seen groups of protection officers and they were taking away survivors at gunpoint and forcing them to raid food stores but he had not seen even them in since August. I explained in brief about the communities we had and our goals and he seemed very excited by it all. I invited him back to the mobile home for some food and to see if he wanted to head back with me tomorrow and he happily agreed.

Wednesday 16th September

I got to know Stephens story last night, He was a homeless guy with a bit of a drug problem but assured me that he had not used the new synthetic drugs in over two months, mainly because all his dealers were dead but he said he felt better for it, he was 23 years old and had no idea why the dead were not interested in him, I asked him if he had any illnesses and he explained he was born with the HIV virus but it was not a problem because he only had to take one pill a month to keep Aids at bay, as I said earlier it is nothing like the '80s where HIV was a death sentence. I told him the infected were not attacking people with severe illnesses and he smiled saying that he never thought HIV would save his life. I did ask him why he did not read the flyers to which he replied that he could not read very well but he knew how to spell his name. My heart went out to the poor lad, all this time alone thinking there was only him and bad people left, bad people was his term for protection officers. I made us a nice meal that we got from Tesco's and offered him a proper spiff, he looked at me oddly and said there was no way an old bloke like me smoked weed, I had to laugh as I did not see myself as old but I remembered at his age thinking anyone over 40 was an old biddy. We had a few spiffs and broke open one of the bottles of spirits I had liberated on my second Tesco run, bless him, even though he was homeless the drink was not one of his demons and he only had one but the fucker smoked me under the table, he could not get enough of the weed. I told him a lot more about the communities we had and about clearing the Islands, I also told him that if he joined us he would be welcomed with open arms as the immune were a vital asset to us. He jumped at the chance and this morning we set off to St David's. We arrived back and after all the medical checks and examinations at the wall, we went to HQ and registered him. The army officer who took his details explained that accommodation was scarce at the minute and he would have to sleep in a dorm for a while, he did not look happy at this because he has not had human contact in weeks. I took Stephen aside and explained that I was going to see a friend of mine a few miles away on a farm and I was certain that he could put him and if he didn't I could offer him a sofa for the time being.

Thursday 17th September

I need not have worried about Stephen, I took him over to Dave's farm last night and after showing him my haul from Curry's I explained about Stephens's situation and the circumstances how we found each other. Dave was more than happy to put him up but explained to him that he would have to pull his weight in exchange for a roof and good food, Stephen readily agreed and the two hit it off straight away. I stayed for dinner and afterwards Dave gave me a massive package of weed that he had cured over the last two weeks, Stephen's eye lit up at this and Dave explained to him that there was plenty for him to smoke but he would not permit him to be stoned 24/7. I made my excuses to them both and headed home for a much-needed sleep but no before quietly explaining to Dave about Stephens lack of reading skills in case he gave him written lists of chores, Dave is a top bloke and explained that once they got to know each other he would bring up the subject and offer to help him learn his letters. Today is the day of my test results so I headed to the clinic, we were quite lucky to have several Dr's as they were either navy/R.A.F. or army and had survived the crisis. I could tell straight away that it was bad news because Sue's greeting was very subdued towards me, I was right the Dr told me that I had to go for further tests straight away at the new community hospital they had set up, he was certain that my illness had progressed. I headed straight away to the hospital and had an afternoon of further blood tests/X-rays and a cat scan. The results would be in by tomorrow because there were no long massive NHS queues to deal with. There was nothing to do but head home and wait, sue invited me over for supper but I explained that I would not be good company tonight.

Friday 18th September

I got blotto last night and did not get up until after 11am, My appointment at the hospital was an hour away so I fed Max and jumped into the shower, I decided to take Max along and leave him on the leash outside, there was no theft here as a rule and because there were not many dogs about anymore he would love the fuss from passers-by. I was only in the hospital for 25 minutes tops and it was exactly as I suspected, my cancer had turned aggressive and had spread at an incredible rate, I was told that even if chemo was available that it would not help me much. I now had at the most six months left, he spoke about pain relief and quality of life but I already had the info about what meds would help ease the pain and eventually end my life, there was no way I was going to fight this to the bitter end and had decided at my first diagnosis that I would die in my own way and time. I had maybe three months before it would start to really affect my daily life and become extremely painful. The thing is that this did not faze me that much, I knew my life was not numbered in multiple years months ago, I grabbed Max and went for a long walk with him, to be honest, I was more worried about Max than me, We were part of each other's lives in a big way and I would hate him pining for me, anyone who did not have a dog would not understand but they become the most important thing in your life. After a walk I headed to HQ to see what the news was with Jono's unit, I knew the Sergeant behind the desk and he happily told me that everything had gone fine in Buxton and the protection officers had backed down once they realised that the defenseless town was not so defenseless after all. Jono's unit would be heading home the next morning and whilst happy at the news I was also sad. We had become so close and even said the L-word to each other, he will be devastated at the news, he knew I had cancer but assumed I had years to go and treatment such as chemo would be available long before then. I am trying to think positive and the thought that Jono and Max would be with each other after my death comforted me. I headed home for an afternoon kip but as I got there I met Sue, she was not daft and realised straight away from my face about my news, we went inside and after a chat about my news I ended up crying like a baby in her arms. This whole apocalypse thing had actually been a boom for me because before it I had a few friends but only one or two real ones who I could share my thoughts with and now I had many friends who were all real and cared a great deal for me, as I did them. I promised Sue that tonight I would spend with her and we would get stoned. The night went well and we were both excited about seeing our partners tomorrow after they returned from Buxton, I decided to stay over and head home the next morning.

Saturday 19th September

I got home around 10 am after getting some chops from the butchers for Tea with Jono, he should be back by late afternoon and I was pretty excited, I had decided not to tell him about my new diagnosis for a few days because he needed a bit of downtime after the Isle of man and Buxton straight after. I cleaned the flat settled down for his return, around 2pm the doorbell went and I figured Jono had forgotten or lost his keys, I buzzed him in but to my surprise, it was Ian and Sue, I was surprised to see them as Sue was awaiting Ian's return and I assumed they would want together time, I invited them in and asked where Jono was. The look on their faces told me everything and I just wanted to throw them out the flat, Ian told me there had been a stupid fucked up accident, I could see tears in his eyes as he explained that one of the vehicles that Jono was in broke down in a country lane just outside Buxton and whilst it was being repaired Jono had gone to a nearby hedge to relieve himself and an infected had bitten him on the neck from behind, the wound was quite bad and before he could turn, he shot himself in the head. I could not believe what I was hearing and collapsed onto the sofa. Through my tears I asked where his body was because if he was left there I would get direction and go bury him myself, Ian explained that they had brought him back for a proper burial as there was no way they were leaving him alone out there. I was in bits and all I could think of was that I had lost the one person in this world that I loved deeply. Sue explained that she and Ian would arrange the funeral because after the last few days it was the last thing I needed. They also asked if I wanted to stay with them for a while but I declined to tell them I needed some time alone plus I knew they needed time to grieve too as Jono was Ian's best friend in the world.

Sunday 20th September

I have not written in here for the last few days, it was just too hard but today was Jono's funeral, it was a full military affair and well attended, I just wanted to run away and hide but I had to be there for a final goodbye, I very nearly joined him in the grave on Wednesday night. I had the pills and booze laid out on the coffee table but I realised that would be the last thing Jono would have wanted plus Sue and Ian came over several times and I did not answer so Ian threatened to kick in the door. The funeral surprised me a bit because the army Priest started talking about Jono's love for me mine for him, I was a bit miffed at this because in my eyes the priest did not know us at all. I was glad I did not lose the plot against the priest because after the service he came and explained that he knew Jono well and during our time in St David, Jono had visited him several times explaining how happy he was to have met me. I could not contain myself and broke into tears, Sue and Ian rushed over to us and Ian just hugged me until I stopped. I had absolutely no idea what to do with myself now Jono was gone, my only saving bit of sanity was that within months I too would be dead and the pain I felt in my heart would be gone. There was a wake at our local after the service but even though I wanted to drink myself into oblivion I only had the one because I knew I would be leaving ST David's by morning.

Monday 21st September

Last night after the pub I headed to the flat, I could not call it home anymore as I wanted to be away from everything that reminded me of our life together, I know that seems cruel but everything that reminded me of Jono was tearing me apart inside. As soon as I got in I sat down and wrote a really emotional letter to Ian and Sue then packed up all the winter clothes that I had liberated from stores and also some essentials for Max such as worming tablets/spot on and his favourite foods, I also grabbed the weed Dave had given me a few days ago and headed out to the compound with the new electric motor homes, This time I chose a luxury vehicle that even had a wood-burning stove in and headed off, I was not really sure where to but firstly it would be Swansea to get some more provisions. I now had the freedom just to roam, there were no worries about charging the vehicle because as I mentioned the charging stations have their own green power supplies and were dotted all over the country, I know a road trip sounds odd in a post-apocalyptic society but to me, the infected were just part of the scenery if I was not immune I too would be hiding behind the walls of our new communities. I decided that I was going to visit London as I had only been there once as a teenage runaway and fled after one night sleeping rough at kings cross. After stocking up with everything I thought I needed in Swansea I headed to the M4 for the journey into London, I had to stop once for a horde to pass, I decided to head off a slip road and onto a bridge overlooking them rather than just stop on the motorway to let them pass, this was purely down to the smell, the hoard must have numbered in the tens of thousands and it would take a while for them to pass so I decided to stretch my legs with Max, there was a service station nearby so we headed for that. This station like many had a charge point for electric vehicles which meant that the fridges would also work inside. I grabbed a couple of bottles of water and had a look in the back rooms, I found several cases of water which I decided to come back for later. After I had collected the water and charged the motor home I headed back towards London, the rest of the journey was uneventful until I was about ten miles from London, I stopped again to admire the view,   as on the horizon were the towers of the city miniaturized from this distance and it looked so peaceful and reminded me of a view of Nottingham from the A52 near Wharton that I stopped to view once many years ago but without the cloudy haze hanging over it from car fumes. It was now late afternoon and I decided to stay here for the night and explore London tomorrow, even though my head was full of thoughts about the last week I felt excited at going into the city. Around 6pm I saw a convoy of three Lorries heading the way I had come, I was a bit worried because there was no army presence this far south and I thought it could be protection officers, I needed not of worried because there were on the other side of the motorway and I could make good my escape. As they neared the lead vehicle came to a stop and two females got out, I recognised one straight away as Leanne, an immune from ST David's, I walked over to them and Leanne smiled at me. They had been to London to save art treasures from the museums and asked what I was up to, I explained why I had to get out of St David's and was close to tears telling them about Jono, Leanne gave me a massive hug and explained she had no idea because they had been away well over a week. I could see the hurt in Leanne's eyes too as she and Jono were friends. Everyone in her group was immune so she suggested we all stay over at the holiday inn up the road for the night.

Tuesday 22nd September

The hotel last night was locked up but after getting inside it was the perfect place for the night, apart from the dust all the electrics were running because most businesses did not rely on the national grid because it was too fragile and blackouts were still the norm. They had a bar there too plus a massive kitchen with a freezer full of food. I felt at ease with Leanne and we both got sloshed with the rest of her group.

Leanne made me actually smile for the first time in ages telling me that she too fancied Jono and thought she was in with a chance until she heard that we were a couple and in her words was well jell of us. We went our separate ways around 10 this morning but before she went I got another hug and she told me about a group of mainly immune but with non-immune amongst them holed up in Buckingham Palace, I was surprised at this because I thought London and everywhere south of was a dead zone. She explained they were a good lot but not yet ready to join the new communities in Wales because of the suffering they had under the Government and protection officers in London. She was certain though that as winter set in that they would move west and fit in well. I pulled up at Trafalgar square and just sat there watching the infected milling around aimlessly, I smiled to myself thinking that apart from the smell and missing limbs that this could be a normal day for the square in any decade of the last century. Now I was here I was still at a loss of what to do with myself so I decided to go to a little shop off the main drag and grab a tourist map just like any visitor to London. I took my gun just in case but I had nothing to fear as Leanne's group explained they had not seen any signs of protection officer in their week here and the palace lot had assured them that they were long gone. I saw a couple of dogs about but they avoided us as their diet now consisted of rotting flesh and the smaller animals such as rats and squirrels, there was an abundance of cats, they were everywhere but never in groups as they have always been solitary animals. The rest of the day we just walked around aimlessly looking at the sights of London, there were signs of looting but as a rule, most shops were fully stocked with whatever they were selling before the shit hit the fan. I thought I wanted to be alone but once in the city I felt lonely and headed towards Buckingham Palace, I realised during the day I was not running away from society but from the sympathy of others in ST David's.

Wednesday 23rd September

We kipped in the vehicle last night but it was a bit creepy as even though the city was dead it still held noises that freaked me out, cats fighting and dogs barking I could deal with but around 2am there was a piercing scream that could only come from a human. I decided that today I would head to the palace to check out the group there. After a breakfast of tinned food we set off and arrived at the palace by 10 am, as soon as you got near you could tell there were survivors there because all along with the Iron gates and fence there was ply-board attached inside up to the height of 8 feet. I approached the gate and sounded my horn, within a few minutes two guys came out armed with rifles, I could understand being armed after Leanne told me of their troubles with the protection officers, I got out the vehicle with Max and raised my hands in submission whilst they searched the motor home and after they had finished they smiled at me and told me to drop my arms and drive through. One of them jumped in the vehicle with me and told me where to park and smiling also telling me the vehicle stunk of weed. I smiled back to him and told him I had a few last nights. Once inside the compound I parked up and met a few locals, they all seemed really nice and explained I could stay as long as I want, I was a bit shocked that they had not checked me for bites and scratches and asked why the response was that London was deserted of living now and the only people they had met in weeks were immune. I looked up at the palace and was gob smacked at the opulence of it all. I almost pinched myself as I could not believe I was actually here. After a few introductions, I was left alone to go look in the palace itself, It was obvious that most rooms were now living quarters but it was not disorganised at all. The Palace obviously had its own power supply because I could smell amazing odours coming from the kitchen, after a hour of having a good old nose around I headed down to the kitchens and it was a hive of activity, one of the workers asked me if I was new and I explained I had arrived only just over a hour ago, he explained that dinner would be ready around one o'clock and if I wanted to help I could go and help set up some tables on the lawn at the back as they were eating   Alfresco because of the unusually hot weather for September. I headed out and set to work helping, surprisingly several kids were ranging from 4yo to young teenagers playing near the lake, this warmed my heart as kids were pretty scarce nowadays, as soon as they saw Max they headed over as a group to fuss him, Max loved this and as we were in an enclosed space I left him to go and play with them. These people seemed properly chilled and it reminded me of a commune I visited in Somerset many years ago. After we had finished the setting up one of the guys asked if I could help him in the wine cellar, I happily agreed and when we got there I was shocked, even for royalty this place was excessive, the place was climate controlled and in the racks were thousands of bottles of wine, he told me to grab a crate and grab as many white wines as I could because we were having chicken for dinner, I asked how they got hold of fresh chicken in the city and he told me that early after the disaster a group had headed to outlying farms and liberated chickens sheep and beef cattle that now roamed freely in the grounds, he also told me that the supply was limited and they would be looking to relocate shortly. Fresh veg was not an issue as the palace had an extensive kitchen garden, I was really hungry and looking forward to dinner but also felt a bit guilty above using up their foodstuffs. The dinner went well and they even brought out a bowl with a mashed up chicken dinner for Max, it seemed totally normal sitting in a palace in the middle of a dead city eating and drinking in the afternoon sun. After lunch I offered to help with clearing and washing up but was told that I am a guest and I should go and relax in the grounds, I did not need telling twice and headed for the lake to have a spliff, A couple joined me within five minutes asking if I minded sharing with them, I took out my weed and told them to help themselves, they were nice people and we got talking about how they survived. The man told me that he has cancer and Julie his partner was not immune, apparently, they had been a couple for over ten years and he had kept Julie alive by going out and liberating goods for their survival, apparently in the early days it was hell in London as they also had to avoid protection officers as well as the dead. His name was Steve and he told me he only came out of their home during the night because the protection officers were rounding up the immune and forcing them at gunpoint to do their bidding. I had seen this myself in Swansea and told him so, The immune with the protection officers here got their revenge though and after getting guns from dead army personal they fought back and attacked their overseers, once they were in control they ordered the surviving officers to take a few vehicles and leave the city, the immune well outnumbers them and the protection officers were not stupid so headed off. The palace was the idea of the protection officers and was well-founded, I told them most of my story and they asked if it was true that the people in wales were not under the control of the army. I assure them that even though the army had established the communities that people were free there and happy, I also told them that King Charles was alive as well as the princes and that a civilian government was being established but I was certain that we would all be executed for raiding his wine cellar, we all laughed at this and I answered their many many questions about our communities.

Thursday 24th September

I have decided to stay with these people for a few days as

they are really nice decent folks and today I have volunteered to head out with a few immune to raid the outlying industrial estates near the M25 in search for water and foodstuffs, obviously, there is no running water anymore in the capital and they have to make do with bottled, luckily bottled water was in abundance at any warehouse that supplied the superstores. I could see this being an issue for them though if they stayed in the palace long-term. We set off quite early in the electric HGV's so we could make a full day of it, I left Max to enjoy playing with the kids because today was about hard graft and he would just get in the way. We made good time and only had to leave the M25 once when a horde of several thousand was spotted in the distance. We found a decent-sized industrial estate just off junction 20 and to our surprise the security gates to the complex was untouched and locked, this meant we could just go in, close the gates after us and we were free to roam around inside at our leisure. The place was quite a find as there were a few foods and drink warehouses plus the power was on so we could charge up their forklifts which would make our jobs easier. After a few hours, we decided to stop for lunch which consisted of anything we wanted as long as it was tinned or frozen. As long as the wind turbines kept spinning and delivering power frozen food was also in abundance in the warehouses that supplied them but another year down the line and this would not be an option. After lunch, we set back to work and within a few hours, we had filled the two trailers on the HGV's and decided to head home. As soon as we left the compound and locked the gates a vehicle approached us from the M25, inside were several people in uniform, I knew straight away that the only idiots still wearing them were the self-important protection officers and I reached for the pistol I had stashed in my backpack. The officers stopped a few meters away and advanced on foot to talk to the immune in the lead vehicle, I hung back a little but not too far as I wanted to hear what they had to say. The protection officers explained that they were a scout group for a larger force and that they were also on a mission to procure foodstuffs, they told us that the rule of law was not over and that they would take our fully loaded vehicles with them and also take our group into custody for looting. There was no way this was going to happen and I asked a couple of guys near me if they had weapons, I got a smile in return and four guys took out a range of guns from the bed compartment of the second HGV's. I know it was not my place to do this but I approached the officers with the other armed men and pointed my weapon directly at them explaining that they need to put any weapons they have on the ground. Luckily most protection officers were fucking cowards and could only inflict their authority on scared people so they obeyed. I decided to lie and told them that we were from wales and under the protection of the army, they did not seem surprised so I assumed they knew of the efforts in the west. After a few arguments we just left them there by the roadside, you could see the rage in their eyes and faces at being defied and I had to smile. As soon as we got on the M25 we saw the rest of their convoy, luckily for us, they were on the opposite carriageway so we just sped up and passed them, a few shots were fired after us but no one was hurt and we made it back in one piece.

Friday 25th September

Crazy day today, the protection officers must have sent a vehicle to follow us because during the night several mortars were fired at the palace and this morning a group of protection officers had set up outside in armoured vehicles. We were given 24 hours to either surrender or suffer the consequences, I did not think they actually had the manpower to conduct a raid on us but they certainly had the firepower. There was a meeting of the group in the palace and everyone was there, I guessed there must be at least two hundred souls here and just over half of the immune, it was decided unanimously that there would be no surrender but also they could not fight because of the children and elderly amongst them. At this point, I spoke up and explained that they would be more than welcome in wales and that even though they had doubts about the army that they would be welcomed and free to live their lives. There were a few discussions but after a short time it was decided that it was the best choice, during the rest of the day the place was a hive of activity, all their transports were fully charged and they were ready to leave by early evening. The plan was that the two HGV's would head out the gates at speed and ram the two lightly armoured vehicles directly outside and that once the way was clear the convoy would head directly out of London via the side gates and head to wales, I offered to drive one of the HGV's and was thanked but also told that this fight was theirs and I should get my mobile home ready and head west with them. the plan was set but with one exception, if the HGV's were damaged whilst ramming them I would be the last to leave and would pick up the drivers if possible.

Saturday 26th September

The convoy from the palace managed to get away safely but the two drivers of the HGV'S were killed whilst trying to save the others, the first HGV ploughed straight into one of the armoured vehicles and there was a huge explosion which I imagined killed everyone in both. The second HGV was blown up by what I can only imagine was an R.P.G before it even got out the gate, I had to change my plans and headed out the side exit with the rest of them. I hung back a bit to make sure no-one was following them but I guess they were busy trying to figure out what happens because they were not used to people defying them. I stayed with the convoy until we arrived at the M25 services where we had arranged to meet if anyone had gone astray. I Gave them my map for the quickest route to St David's and also a list of the charging stations along the way, I also gave them a letter to give to HQ partly explaining that the protection officers were still a problem in the south and also a personal letter to give to Ian and Sue, once the army knew about the situation down here it would be easy for them to locate the protection officers bases and hopefully destroy them. I was not ready to head back to wales yet and I said my goodbyes and headed to the junction for the M1, I think I might end up back in wales shortly but for now, I had decided to head to the east midlands, partly to visit my home city and see my home but also just to be alone again for a while.

Sunday 27th September

Yesterday as I approached junction 15a I noticed a thick column of smoke on my right and wondered what had occurred, I decided that I now had all the time in the world to have a look and headed off the junction in the direction of Northampton, after a few minutes' drive I crested a hill and there in the distance was the entire city center ablaze, it was like something out of an apocalypse film, every tower and every building I could see from here was well and truly alight. I looked down at the roads leading out of the city and saw what looked to me like a black smudge spreading outwards, I had no idea what this was and decided to get closer, I got within a mile or so and realised the smudge was thousands upon thousands of charred infected stumbling away from the blaze. If I had not known about the communities in wales and on the Isle of Man plus probably other islands by now, I would have thought that humanity was finished. I cannot describe the sight and smell and I just sat there with tears streaming down my face. Max picked up on my mood and came and gave my face the biggest licking. I decided to move away from the city and headed off the main drag towards the countryside and Kettering, I knew I could use the back roads and maybe head to Oakham at some stage to check on the lot at ST Georges barracks. We stopped on a quiet country lane for a bite to eat and decided to park up for the rest of the day and take Max for a good walk.

Monday 28th September

We set off early and headed towards Oakham via Kettering and Corby, we were not on the road long when I witnessed more smoke on the horizon in the direction of Kettering, I had a sick feeling in my stomach and as we got closer my fears were confirmed, Kettering was well and truly alight just like Northampton, there was no way this could be a coincidence but there was nothing to do but skirt around the town and carry on with my journey, after we had bypassed the town and heading towards Corby I noticed what I assumed was alone infected walking along the road, as I neared I realised that this person was too sure-footed to be infected and must be immune or very brave/stupid. I stopped and asked him if everything was ok, the guy looked disheveled and wide-eyed and said everything was fine but would I give him a lift to Corby, I was a bit concerned for his mental state but agreed to take him as it was only a few miles away. As soon as he sat down in the passenger seat he started ranting about god's judgment and this was the biblical Armageddon. I had met god squads before and knew better to interrupt or argue with him so I just let him carry on, Max obviously did not like him and headed to the bedroom at the back. after a few miles the guy started raising his voice and stating that God had told him to cleanse the cities and towns with fire, I clicked straight away he was responsible for the fires and seriously thought about stopping there and then to make him walk but I realised that this mad man could, in theory, destroy many towns and cities with his craziness. After a mile or so I pulled into a layby explaining that I had to take a leak and stretch my legs, I went into the back living area with the excuse that I wanted a cigarette from my jacket. I instead went into one of the draws and took out the pistol I had and headed outside. The guy was obviously happy to have an audience to his ranting and followed me out, I am not proud of my next action, I took out the pistol and shot him in the head because I knew that with communities in the west the cities would be a valuable resource for certain items in the future and some may even be resettled. I immediately puked up the contents of my stomach and could not stop retching for a minute or so. I did feel really bad but what choice did I have? I justified my actions by telling myself this guy could have made it all the way to wales and caused a lot of problems for the remaining population. I did not fancy driving anymore because I was shaking like a leaf but there was no way I was staying here with his corpse lying in the grass. I decided to head straight on to Oakham and the barracks just outside the town. I made pretty good time and arrived in Oakham by 11am, the town was deserted of people living or otherwise buy most of the barricades were still up and once I had navigated through one I decided to have a look around, the town had basically been stripped of everything worthwhile, even the books in the library had gone, I knew there was an organised evacuation here because the Army were in radio contact with wales and had told them about moving to the barracks, I headed over to the former R.A.F and was surprised to see this deserted too except for a couple of lorries and a few guys in army uniform. I got to the gate and sounded my horn and two of the lads ran up and opened it. I got out and spoke to them, it appears that the main population had only left for wales the day before and this lot were just tying up loose ends. I told them I was from wales but had left a while ago but not before we had cleared one of the islands, they explained that now the isle of white and most of the jersey isles were now safe and many of the population had relocated to there, so there was now room in St David's and St Asaph for the people who were here. I stayed for an hour or so helping them load up and then headed out to Rutland water to park up for the rest of the day.

Tuesday 29th September

I got totally shit-faced last night at the reservoir but not in a good way, I could not stop thinking of the guy I killed yesterday, for me, there was no other way of seeing it but murder, no matter what justification I told myself I had killed a man in cold blood. It was weird sitting in the car park with amazing views of the water and countryside but not even noticing it. The only thing I noticed was the amount of dead walking in groups across the fields, this in itself was odd after wales and the lack of infected in the countryside there. I remember hearing the news that most of the midlands farms were either overran or evacuated because the towns and cities were just too numerous here and the dead had spread out into every place. I honestly think that like the city infected (sticking to the cities and motorway) that townspeople who became infected stuck to the countryside, plus there were not many company farms with security here because if food became a problem again they would be within walking distance of looters. Several hundred bodies were floating in the reservoir, I had no idea why but I knew that once submerged in the water the infected truly died. I had a hangover today and even though the roads were clear I decided to spend another day here, I took Max out for a long walk and tried to keep my mind off yesterday. By mid-afternoon I was beginning to feel more myself and decided to nip up to Stamford to see if I could scrounge up a decent meal, I knew Stamford was entirely run on green energy because the government made a song and dance about it a few years ago so looting aside I should be able to find something. I had food in the vehicle but it was dried stuff like pasta and packet soups. It only took 20 mins to get there and to my surprise, the place looked untouched by anything. All the shops were locked up tight but intact and there was no infected in the streets at all. I could not explain it but it was a pleasant surprise. First thing first, I broke into newsagents because I had run out of cigarettes.   I went up to the flat upstairs to see if there was any clue to where the townspeople had gone but I could not find anything. On the way out of the shop I noticed a local paper sitting in piles on the counter, the headline was that all residents were ordered to Burghley house which was now a high-security walled protection officers academy a few miles away, it also stated this was for their own protection but I doubted that, but also knew everyone would be too afraid not to go anyway. I knew the house well because as a kid at school near Oakham, we used to go there because the grounds held an adventure playground. I decided to head straight over there even though it belonged to the protection officers, if there were any left I knew I could blag them if I met any or at worst play along with them and offer help. As I neared the estate I had to wind up the window because of the smell, I knew it would not be good because I had smelled the same thing multiple times over the last few months. I stopped the vehicle very close to the wall and climbed on the roof to get a look, the sight I was appalling, there were miles of razor-wire fences with tens of thousands of truly dead people with a few thousand infected inside, beyond the inner fence and between it and the wall was a few hundreds of infected protection officers. I'm not sure but to me, it seemed that the latter had imprisoned and murdered the population of Stamford here and had succumbed to the virus themselves. I could see the house itself in the distance but it was nothing more than a shell now, It looked as if it had burnt down months ago, there were still several horses and deer in the grounds beyond the fenced enclosure going about their business as usual. Once again it made me think that nature actually has a chance to thrive. There was nothing for me to do here and part of me was pleased that at least these infected were locked up tight and would just rot away without causing any further damage. I headed back to Stamford and decided to have a hair of the dog at one of the pubs in the main street. Even though the electrics were on I decided to have a bottled beer rather than from the tap just in case. The beer was ice cold as it had stood in the fridge for months now and the sell-by date was well into next year. I grabbed some bar snacks too and water for Max and headed outside to sit at the benches out front. It was another pleasant day and the sun was still shining, I did wonder if that was down to global warming but to be fair I did not care anymore, we sat there for a good hour and I grabbed Max some food from the vehicle. I even managed to roll a spliff and sat there quite stoned when suddenly I heard dogs barking in the distance, after five minutes a few deer ran up the main street in terror followed by a pack of dogs, I had seen a lot of the aftermath of the infection but this was the first time I had seen more than one or two dogs wandering about. There must have been at least twenty of them racing after the deer and before I could react they had disappeared up the street. There were two that obviously could not keep up with the pack and started to approach us snarling and barking, this time I did not have any second thought and took out the gun and shot the lead dog, the other looked totally surprised and scurried off with its tail between his legs. I was going to walk to the shopping precinct but thought better of it now and grabbed max and headed back to the vehicle. I really thought the bigger stores would have been looted by the protection officers but I guess the infection had taken them by surprise at Burghley because there were an ASDA and Tesco totally untouched at the edge of town, I left Max in the vehicle this time whilst I went in and grabbed the makings of a nice meal. The freezers were all working and I grabbed us both a rump steak with some tinned potatoes and veg plus a bottle of wine, I even got a frozen cheesecake for after. I decided not to stay in the town any longer because I now feared for the safety of Max with the wild dogs so I headed back to the reservoir for the night.

Wednesday 30th September

I made an early start today and decided to head to Derby via the A606 and Nottingham. The journey was uneventful except when I entered Melton Mow Mowbray and saw a group of five people running out of the town towards me, I was a bit surprised and stopped, they approached me very cautiously and asked who I was and where I was heading, I noticed that a group of infected was a few hundred yards away and I could see the fear in their faces, there was no way these people were infected so I told them to jump in the back and we could find a safer place to park up and talk. They happily agreed and we set off through the town towards Nottingham, after a few miles I pulled over and we shared stories, apparently, they had two immunes with them up to about a week ago but one day they went out to forage/loot the town and never came back so they decided to head out of their farmhouse just outside town to find food and water, they had no idea how bad things were and were shocked at the amount of infected and within hours they were virtually surrounded by them and had to run for it, they really had no idea where to run to but had heard from the two immunes that Oakham had isolated itself with the help of the army and they would try to get there, I asked why they had not done so sooner but they explained that they were afraid of any sort of authority because they had seen the protection officers killing non-infected months ago. I explained that Oakham was no longer viable as a safe haven but the army was not like the protection officers and they were actively saving people, I told them about wales and the islands and two of the men burst into tears, they had no idea that communities had survived and thought there were just isolated survivors like them dotted around or worse still groups under the law of the protection officers or army. I had to explain again about the army not being their enemies but they still seemed unsure. After a few discussions, I offered to take them with me to Derby and find them some transport to head to wales. They agreed but I knew it would take a bit more to convince them about the army being good guys. I had to think on my feet as there was no way we would all fit comfortably in my old flat, then I remembered Rebecca who I met almost at the start of the troubles, her dad was a bigwig in the government and they had a walled home in Darley with the new solar panels that could run an entire houses electrics. We decided to go straight through Nottingham without stopping, the place was a mess with thousands of infected just roaming aimlessly from street to street, we had to stop once on the ring road for them to pass us by as there was no way to double back at the time, the people in the back were terrified with the infected right outside but I assured them that unless they were seen there would be no trouble from them.

Thursday 1st October

We arrived in Derby by mid-afternoon and headed straight to the house in Darley, the gates were still closed and untouched so we went in, after closing the gate and having a quick look around I told the others it was safe to come out. I explained how I had found this place and told them that the electrics were fully working and they could take a shower if they wanted, I knew even after all this time that there was a good water supply because this place was built for defense and had its own rainwater collectors on the roof. I left them to it and headed inside, apart from the dust the place was untouched since my last visit so I knew the food would not be an issue because the freezers were full when we left months ago. My old flat was only a few miles away so I decided to head over there in the camper, no way was I heading out on foot after seeing the wild dogs in Stamford. The area looked untouched except for the litter, I knew this was no longer my home and never would be but it was nice to be back and Max obviously was pleased as he ran straight to the communal door and wagged his tail, we went in and the flat was fine except there was obviously rats living here now, their shit was all over the place and my old sofa was ripped and seemed to be their nest, I had romantic ideas of coming home and dying here but they all went out of my head after looking around. There was no point in staying so I grabbed Max and took him to the local park which was once his daily walking place, he was so pleased to be back and just ran around happy as Larry barking, we stayed for an hour or so then decided to head back to the camper, on the way we saw three dogs heading our way and I got a bit scared because I left the pistol in the vehicle, the dogs approached stealthily and once they were within ten feet I recognised them as Mick's dogs which I had set free back in July, Max started barking as he really disliked two of them and even though he is a Shih Tzu, they were scared of him. The dogs started wagging their tales as soon as they recognised me and after putting Max on his lead I went over to greet them, they were fine except they were very skinny, I decided that I was not going to leave them here and took them to the camper to feed them and give them water, Max was not pleased but it was something he knew he had to deal with and chose to ignore the two he did not like. I took the dogs back with me intent on telling the others that they would take them to Wales with them, they owed me after all. When we got back the dogs took to the people straight away and I knew they would be going with them without me asking.

Friday 2nd October

I decided to go to the industrial estates near pentagon island where I first got a vehicle at the start of all this shit, it was a few miles but I decided to walk because it would be pointless driving and leaving the camper just to bring another one back, the people I picked up in Melton could not drive, they explained that there was no point in learning because they could never afford to run one in the economy we had, I suppose I am lucky because I passed in 95 way before Brexit and things were simpler and the country was doing ok. I set off around 10 leaving Max to happily play with Buffy, the one dog of micks that he liked. I decided to go through town because I wanted to grab a few winter jumpers and coats, the weather was turning now, not sure if it is my age or cancer but I was definitely feeling it. The town was deserted except for cats, there seemed to be hundreds of the fuckers roaming about, I did not dislike them but I have always been a dog person. Derby was one of the first towns to get green energy and lots of the town Centre had power still so I popped in newsagents and grabbed some bottled water and energy bars plus some cigarettes and then headed to the Intu Centre, it was strange entering the shopping Centre, there were only a few infected roaming about but my hairs were on end because I loved watching zombie flicks in the past and good old George A. Romero loved his shopping centers. I had to smile because my goose pimples were down to the first time I ever felt truly scared when watching the original dawn of the dead. I actually sat down on the seats in the middle of the walkway and laughed at the surrealism of it all. I headed towards Blacks the camping store on the upper floor, I was a bit shocked to find a couple of infected up here because I knew they could not do stairs and wondered how they managed. This place looked like it had just shut for the night, there was no windblown litter and the place looked normal. I had to break the glass to the camping store and to be fair I felt a bit guilty because I had destroyed the look of normality of the place, no problem finding my size because after months of being on the road and some hard graft plus cancer I was now in better physical looking shape than I have ever been. I grabbed what I needed and headed out towards the rear entrance (no pun intended). on my way I heard a sharp ping and looked up to see the lift door open and an infected stumble out, I smiled again thinking that explained how they got upstairs, I wondered actually how long a life the wind turbines actually had, I imagined that barring faults that their lifespan must be in decades and by then wales and the Islands will be well established and teaching the next generation of kids how to replace or repair them but to be fair the army and navy had plenty of engineers if anything went wrong in the communities with regards to power/water. I left my shopping bags at the exit and continued on to the industrial units. It was actually a really nice walk on a fairly nice autumnal day, I even stopped off for a spliff by the river on the way. I found a suitable camper van that would fit all five of them and it was electric so all I had to do was head back and give them directions which I knew had adequate charger points. They seemed nice enough but I still needed my own space and the only company I wanted at the minute was Max. After charging the vehicle I headed back to the house via picking up my shopping I had left earlier. I arrived back to the smell of food being cooked and it smelt really nice, one of the women had found a veg plot in the garden with carrots and peas in the greenhouse and decided to cook a roast beef dinner, the only thing missing was Yorkshire pudding because there were no eggs. We cracked open some wine and after food, we made plans for their travel the next day, I had already decided that I was not going back yet, I would eventually but I still needed me-time. I feel a bit selfish but I had no responsibilities so why shouldn't I think of me.   We stayed up late discussing plans and several times they suggested I should join them but I got the feeling they only wanted me to come along to minimise the risk to them when they needed to charge the camper.

Saturday 3rd October

They set off early with the three dogs happily joining them and after they had left and I closed the gates I actually breathed a sigh of relief, last night got pretty heated and they felt it was their right to take me along with them in case things went tits up. They proper pissed me off to the point where I explained that I owned a gun and anyone ordering me to do things against my will would face the working end of it. I was not joking either, if they had tried their luck with me, I would have used the fucker. As soon as they had gone I headed back to bed for a few hours, the house was warm and cosy and I intend to stay around here for a while. I think my illness was getting the better of me too because I was always feeling tired and I taking painkillers almost daily now. We slept almost the entire day away and awoke early evening, I was a bit pissed off at this because I wanted to grab some more supplies for Max today. I let him out in the garden to explore and do his thing and headed into the tv room where I knew the former owner had an extensive digital collection of movies and music. The man was totally anal, everything was in alphabetical order and there was some pretty good shit here, I skipped the walking dead and the entire Z section but found pink Floyds the wall and fully intended to chill out with a spliff and some whiskey later watching it after a long soak with some of the pure essential oils I found in the bathroom.

Sunday 4h October

I woke up this morning without a care in the world, it is amazing what a good bath and a nice night's sleep do for the spirit, not to mention the spliff and single malt. I was at a loose end and after the last few months, it felt amazing to not have anything to do, of course, my thoughts were free too and went straight to Wales and the loss of Jono. I also missed some of the true friends I had met but I was not one to dwell as I knew in my heart that eventually, I would head back to them before I truly succumbed to cancer. I grabbed some breakfast and decided to head on foot with Max to the Kingsway shopping precinct where I knew they had a pet superstore. The day was amazing for October and I think they walk was doing us both good. After about a hour we arrived and to my surprise, I saw two guys park up in a van and head towards the Sainsbury's store, they were obviously immune as they had walked straight past a group of infected. I shouted over to them and they responded with both hand raised. I went over to them to talk and Max ran in front obviously excited to see them. As I neared I recognised them as the two junkies from the few days of the crisis, I had to search for the name of the one I had known from years ago, I was certain it was Steve. He recognised me straight away and smiled. They looked different and I told them so, they both smiled and explained that they were no longer using much brown (heroin) and soon got bored with drugs after realising that there was no one stopping them using anymore. Plus they had met several non-immune including children who they now foraged for and kept safe. This warmed my heart and I offered to help them gather some supplies. After a few hours collecting food and medicine we decided to sit down on the benches and have a cold beer from the still working fridges and even though I had walked, I still bought an eighth of weed with me. They were not out to get drunk but explained a few beers and driving was not a biggy now because there was no one else driving. They explained that for the first few weeks they just got out of their heads after finding all the gear they needed at their former dealer's homes, they smiled explaining that one dealer who was in their words a dirty nonce actually showed the first bit of charity in his life after intentionally overdosing by leaving a note explaining where his very large stash was hidden. After a month they came across a non-immune teenage girl foraging for food in the same Sainsbury's where we had just shopped and she was in a terrible state having been cornered in the store by the infected and not being able to return with vital food and water to her other family members and a few people who had all took refuge in a local nursery, this made me smile at the ingenuity of the survivors because Protection officers stations/public buildings and schools were the only really safe places where you could survive because they all now had high fences and security gates, I imagined that not many sought out the stations as refugees because they knew that some things are worse than death and being at the mercy of the protection officers was one of them, public building such as museums/courts and so on would probably be shut up tight but schools would have been perfect because the fences were only there to stop wrong'uns out during school hours and the main entrances were usually open but with guards and cameras protecting them. They told me they drew the infected away by setting off a car alarm at the far end of the car park and rescued the girl, she was grateful but very nervous because of their disheveled appearance, after a lengthy convo with the girl the guys decided to man up (their words) and charged up one of the supermarkets delivery vans and filled it with food to take to the survivors, their intention was just to drop off the food but after meeting the others and seeing young children suffering they decided to stay and help, within a week of so they realised that the nursery was just too small for the forty or so survivors so they went to the arriva bus depot and got a bus and moved them all to to the hall in Markeaton park on the outskirts of the city, the hall and park had long beedn enclosed by high fences and security cameras because a few years ago it was used as the rallying point for antigovernment protests because all city centres had banned large congregations and the penalties for breaking that law was minimum 2 years in prison and the bastards had sent thousands down.   I knew that they all had their own wind turbine there that supplied power to the park and surrounding villages and to give the guys credit they chose well. The hall supplied all the living quarters they needed and the survivors had converted the orangery into a massive greenhouse plus the kids had space to be kids and had a playground and boating lake at their disposal. I asked them why they had not moved to Wales because I knew Derby had been targeted with leaflets from the air force. They told me they had read them but were afraid it was a scam by the protection officers and there was no way they were falling for it. I knew exactly how they felt but explained some of my stories and told them it was safe, I could see the relief in their faces and a few tears in their eyes told me of the stress they had been under protecting the others, I had felt exactly the same over the last few months. I also told them that the monthly drug for HIV sufferers was readily available there and they had hospitals up and running. I decided to head back to the house but promised them that I would pop over to them tomorrow and retell my story to the others. I left them with an eighth of weed and headed off but not before I

told them about David and his abundance of weed in his
Polly tunnels.

Monday 5th October

I got back around 4pm yesterday and was shocked to see a
protection officers van outside the gates to the house, my
first instinct was to run but I knew I could blag it because all I
had to do was play into their sense of superiority and treat
them like saviours, intelligence was not the main
requirement when applying to become one of them in the
past, all you needed was to be small-minded and anti-social. I
approached cautiously and saw a man and woman sitting
inside, the woman seemed familiar and Max ran straight up
to the van tail wagging. The woman smiled and opened her
window a bit. I could see why they had not left the van as
there were a group of infected on the other side. She greeted
me by name and it dawned on me that it was Rebecca whose
father had actually owned the house. I walked about 50 feet
down the road and started shouting and broke a car window
to get the attention of the mob, they all turned as one and
headed towards me and as soon as they got close they
started to ignore me so I ran back to the gates and opened
them for the vehicle to get in safely. Once safe they both got
out the van and Rebecca got out and hugged me. I happily
took the hug even though we did not know each other well
my first instinct when meeting her months ago was that she
was a nice person. I invited them in then explained how

stupid I felt doing so because after all, it was her home, she laughed it off and introduced her friend as Colin. I made us all a cup of tea even though after the beer at Sainsbury's I wanted another. I asked why they were here in Derby because the last I knew, she had joined the army convoy going north to Scotland. She explained that for the last few months she had been living there but now with Wales partially clear and the islands free of infected the army had decided to return to the communities south of the border, she explained that at first, the people were not happy having the British army on their soil but things soon changed when they realised that they were not an invading force but there to help, the communities in Scotland which were numerous now had stability and their own very small government which now wanted to return to the united kingdom because mainland Europe no longer existed as a political entity or even as a safe place to live, there had been no word from them in months even though we were receiving messages from further afield. This still did not explain why they were in Derby but I was willing to wait for a reason without asking. She then explained that it was pure folly why they were here, Colin was her partner and she had told him that if they were going to Wales or the Islands permanently she would like to get some personal belongings so they could really call their new place home. I just smiled broadly at her because I had done exactly the same thing at my old flat few days ago, my smile was also because of the fact that two non-immune had possibly risked their lives for memories. I think I said earlier in this diary how attractive Rebecca was and Colin had no chance but to say yes when she flashed that winning smile. Rebecca asked if she could cook us all a final meal in her home because she was certain she would never visit again, I felt a bit embarrassed saying yes because we both knew I had no right to be here. We went in and Rebecca headed straight to the kitchen, I offered Colin a drink and we went into the main living room, I had left the heating on so it was nice and cozy, Colin seemed like a nice bloke but I was still worried that he may have been a protection officer because of the vehicle they arrived in, as soon as we settled down and Max had jumped on his knee for a fuss I asked him outright about the vehicle, he must have sensed my meaning behind it and instantly put my mind at rest by explaining that the vehicle they set off in from Scotland had broken down just south of Leeds on the M1 and they had to trek on foot to the nearest services which were a few miles away, he told me that they walked along the fast lane because it offered safety and a good view of their surroundings. they made the services without seeing any infected and the services were also deserted except for two infected protection officers, he explained that they must have been infected recently because their uniforms were instantly recognising and most infected these days were virtually naked with their former clothes hanging off in rags after being in the open in all weather in these last few months. They dispatched the infected and after looking around they found the vehicle still plugged into a charging station. He assumed that the two they had killed stopped to charge it and were caught off guard, after getting some bottled water they headed straight off towards derby but on the way, they came across two vehicles heading north but as soon as they saw the protection officers van they increased speed and headed off one of the junctions. He told me that he could not blame them because if he came across people in one of the official vehicles he too would have fled. I smiled at this and decided I liked Colin, we chatted for a while then Rebecca came back and poured herself a drink explaining that we were having fish/chips and peas for tea. Rebecca it seems had struck lucky up north and apart from the two infected they saw on their way down here, she had not seen any infected in months because she was doing admin for the army tucked safely behind the walls in Eyemouth. Colin on the other hand had risked his life on numerous occasions volunteering to forage with the immune, he hated the infected with a vengeance and was not scared to admit it. I told them most of my story but leaving out my relationship with Jono, the last thing I needed was sympathy. I also explained about the group in Markeaton Park and that I was popping over tomorrow because I think after hearing from someone in the know about Wales that they may be moving there.   I offered them along but explained that we would go in my camper van because the last thing I wanted to do is turn up in a protection officers van, they happily agreed and I suggested to Rebecca that we have a spliff and settle down for the evening, I knew she smoked it because I had shared a joint with her months ago when we first met. Colin it seems was not adverse to it either and we got quite stoned. The meal was great but I think the fact we all had munchies made it seem better. By nine I was not far off being shitfaced and feeling really tired so I left them listening to some music and headed off to bed.

Tuesday 6th October

I decided this morning to give my luxury camper van to Rebecca and Colin, I will miss it but I noticed plenty of them on the Garage forecourts in the industrial units near pentagon island a few miles away and it will be easy to pick up another upgraded electric one any time I wanted. I helped them pack it with some of Rebecca's personal stuff and we headed out to Markeaton park by mid-morning. When we arrived I was shocked at the amount of infected lined along the fence near the main gate and realised that we would have to draw them away before we could safely enter. It was easy enough to do and became second nature to me over the last few months, we stopped on the A38 about 600 yards away and I pipped the horn continuously whilst Rebecca and Colin went on the roof to shout, we slowly lead them well away from the gate and doubled back, the gate was opened as soon as we neared and locked as soon as we entered. We went straight to the hall and was greeted by the community, the place was neat and tidy and they all seemed friendly enough, I saw Steve coming down the stairs and went to ask him about the build-up of infected at the fence, he explained that every time someone came or went from the park that more infected appeared, they did know about blocking the view from the infected but they did not have the manpower to complete the entire fence or even part of it, they did try initially with a cloth and some MDF but it was October and the winds had blown most away. I introduced Rebecca and Colin and explained they were on their way west into wales, Steve explained that he had talked to the community and although there were a few that were still doubtful the rest of them were in the process of packing and intended leaving the next day, I was asked if I could talk to the whole community at lunch just to reassure them about the army. I happily agreed and asked if any help was needed. I was assured everything was in hand so I went out and explored the park, this place was well-founded, not too far from the city itself and it had easy access to the ring road and the A38 but anyone here long term would eventually run into trouble because even from here I could see damage on parts of the fence. After a hour or so I and Max headed back to the hall, as we entered there was a lovely smell of chicken coming from the kitchen, Lunch was in ten minutes apparently so my timing was spot on. The lunch was amazing, the chickens they raise themselves and all the veg was fresh produce from their converted orangery. I will not go into the details of what I told them about Wales but I really emphasized how there was no discrimination or protection officers there, by the time I had finished the room was full of smiles and I even got a round of applause to which I know I turned bright red. It was decided there and then that the whole community would be setting off at 9am the next day.

Wednesday 7th October

Everything went smoothly this morning, I think some of the
community were surprised I was not going with them but I
didn't bother explaining why. I stayed at the hall for a few
hours after seeing the last of the convoy head out and had a
look around, there was plenty of veg and fruits still growing
in the converted orangery and I decided to take some at a
later stage. I have left a crappy old model electric car but
decided to leave the thing there and after securing the main
gate we took a slow walk back to the house in Darley. I know
I wanted space from people but that walk back was the
loneliest I had ever felt in my life, not even a cat stirred and
isolation overwhelmed me. I noticed the five lamps and even
though it was locked up tight, there was a light on
downstairs, the light did not mean life like it did pre-green
energy but I knew it means that the fridges/freezers would
be working, It was easy enough to enter without much
damage and apart from the dust this place seemed as if it
would be open for business at the drop of a hat, I was not
hungry or in need of alcohol but I just fancied sitting there
with a glass of coke and a spliff, this made me smile because I
was actually barred from this very pub in March for smoking
a blunt in the beer garden. I found the jukebox and luckily it
was free to play, I suppose I could have got change from the
till if it was not and this made me smile again because I
honestly never thought I would need money again, I left Max
in the pub for a few minutes whilst I popped across the road
to smileys off license/grocery store. The door was not locked

and I knew why they chap who used to run the store was a devout Hindu and would have left it open on principle after it all went to shit just so people could take what they need. It looked like hardly anyone had entered because most produce was still on the shelves. The place did not smell bad so I assume Mr. Khan had removed all the perishables and either left or was dead upstairs in his flat, there was no way I was going to look plus it was none of my business. I grabbed some bottled water for Max and some dog food and headed back to the pub. I was only gone five mins but Max acted as if I had been gone all day. I fed and watered him then sat down to an ice-cold coke and started making a spliff. I almost shit myself when a voice shouted that I could not smoke that shit in the bar, I looked up and to my surprise and pleasure, Mr Khan stood there smiling at me. I was gob smacked, to say the least, and went over to shake his hand, I was never so pleased to see anyone in my life, I knew his given name was Irfan but out of respect I always referred to him as Mr. Khan, I have known him since moving to Derby and on one of our first meetings he had captured a shoplifter in his shop who had stolen some tins of food, I remember clearly him telling the thief that if it had been alcohol he was stealing that the police would be called but as it was food, the thief could take the goods with him and if he ever needed food this badly again in the future that he could come back and would be given stuff near it's sold by date. I have held him in high respect ever since. He grabbed a bottled lager and joined me, Max was straight on his knee because he had known him since being a 12-week old puppy. We chatted for a while and he told me his story, since the start of it all he had stayed shut up in the flat upstairs from the shop with his wife, waiting for word from their daughter at Durham uni who had told them she was going to defy the travel ban and head home, luckily the shop was running off the wind turbines outside the city, so staying warm and cooking was not an issue, they occasionally popped downstairs for foodstuff and bottled water. They had run out of water in the first month or so and headed across to the pub, he found one of the doors at the back unlocked and the place deserted, after discovering the freezers full and virtually an unlimited supply of water for two people in the basement he decided to stay over here whilst keeping an eye on his shop. I asked about his wife but he explained that soon after they had set up in the pub that his wife and he went back to the flat to get some personal things and on the way back his wife was attacked and bitten, he successfully fought off the attacker and destroyed him by repeated blows to the head using the cricket bat he kept behind the counter. His wife Udyati was putting on a brave face but they both knew what a bite meant, after securing his wife in the pub Irfan went off to the pharmacy on Keddleston road around the corner to get ant-biotic and bandages, he told me he had to break in and felt so guilty that he left a note explaining his actions and who he was, on the way back he was attacked himself and bitten, I was shocked at this because it was weeks ago but let him continue, He arrived back at the pub and told me that he actually felt relieved that he would die with his wife. He nursed her for almost a full day before she passed away, he knew that she did not want to return as the infected so he gently entered a screwdriver deep into her eye socket, by this time tears were streaming down his face but he continued. He knew he did not have long and went into the enclosed car park and built a pyre from the benches and other wood from the building, the Co-op garage was right next door and was fully powered so after finding the pump switches he collected enough fuel to dowse the pyre and returned to lay he wife to rest respectfully. After the pyre, he had taken a bottle of whiskey to the bedroom and locked himself in so that when he returned he could not hurt anyone. He drank most of the whiskey and collapsed because as a rule, he did not drink, he explained that he had slept almost the entire day and woke up feeling terrible, putting it down to the infection he went back to sleep waking hours later and feeling an intense hunger, He let himself out of the bedroom and made himself a good vegetarian meal from the freezers. He looked at his wound and there was no sign of infection around the bite. He had no idea what was happening because within a hour of Udyati being bitten the infection had spread almost the entire length of her arm. After taking some strong anti-biotic over a few days he realised that he was going to survive or at least take much longer to succumb to infection. As the days became weeks and then months he just stayed at the pub watching the flat for any sign of his daughter, he told me he knew in his heart that she would not be coming but he had nowhere else to go, he had contemplated ending his life on several occasions but his religion was too strong to let him violate the code of ahimsa (non-violence) therefore suicide was equally as sinful as murdering another. He had also had never learned to drive so leaving was pointless. I honestly did not know what to say to him, throughout all of this I had not suffered a quarter of what he and many others had and I still feel guilty about it. I gave him a bit of insight of why I was in derby and offered him to come to the house with me, obviously, he was not immune to attacks so I told him I would go to the hall in Markeaton park and pick up the vehicle left for me. It was agreed that we would stay here for the night and I would set off first thing tomorrow, the reason being that he had some packing to do and he would cook us up an amazing last meal here. Irfan may have been a good religious man (not a combination that comes up much) but boy could he drink, he avoided the hard stuff but must have drunk his weight in bottled and canned beer during that evening, he was true to his word and cooked an amazing veg curry for himself and a chicken one for me, he did say there was beef if I wanted but I was not going to offend him by asking him to cook what was to him a sacred animal.

Thursday 8th October

I set off early to the hall, it was only a mile or so away so I left Max with Irfan and they both seemed happy with that, I collected the vehicle and headed back with no drama and after we had packed up his few personal items I suggested we go back to the hall and help ourselves to some fresh veg and fruit, plus I wanted Irfan to actually be able to feel the wind in his hair after months of virtually being a prisoner in the pub. After we had arrived at the hall and re-secured the gates after us I told Irfan I would park up at the hall and he and Max could walk down to me or wander around the park if he wanted, the joy in his face almost made me shed a tear and he happily agreed. I left them both to it after first giving Irfan Max's favourite ball from my pocket, it was a couple of hours before they joined me at the hall and I did not mind one bit because I could only imagine how the freedom to roam meant after his self-imposed captivity. When they entered the hall Irfan came and hugged me and also thanked me for letting him take time to himself in the open air. He was not a stupid man and saw that I was giving him space right away. We went into the orangery and took what we needed, I was tempted to try and catch a chicken that the community had released before heading to Wales but even though they were all staying near their old hutches my chasing days were long gone. The day was nice so I grabbed a couple of bottles of water and asked Irfan to sit with me outside. I had to fill him in on the whole picture about Wales and the Islands plus to tell him the unique situation he was in, I had never met or heard of anyone surviving a bite. I will not go into details because my story is already written here but Irfan listened to every word intently and when I had finished he explained that he must get to Wales and the scientist/Dr's and offer himself for tests if it could help others, I knew he would do that because even though we were not close friends, I knew his character. This left me with a dilemma of my own, I did not want to return to wales yet but Irfan could not drive but it was vitally important that he get to the specialist to be examined. I knew that ultimately I had no choice in the matter and told him that I would take him west. The rest of the day went as expected, we locked the gate and headed to Darley. Once within the gates of the house, I told Irfan to treat the place as home whilst I would head out to the industrial estates to get us another electric motor home, I would be looking for an expensive top of the range model again because I figured we may as well go in style. I told Irfan that tomorrow I would head off to get a suitable vehicle and asked if there was anything he fancied bringing back, he seemed hesitant to say something but I reassured him that there was no danger outside for me so whatever he needed I could get. He explained that he had no winter clothes and in his sherwani's he was freezing his bollocks off, I smiled at this and asked his sizes, it would be an easy task to pick him up what he wanted. He offered to make us another meal this evening and told me he had found some nice wine when he was looking around the house. I was never a wine guy and decided to head out to the local grocery store that I knew had the power to grab some coke to go with the whiskey I was going to consume later. The shop run took all of ten minutes and I noticed that many of the infected were just standing in the same spot, I had no idea why until I also noticed a puddle had an icy coating on its surface. It clicked straight away that we had reports from the Nordic countries that they became almost dormant in the cold.   I headed back to the house looking forward to a nice meal and to get a bit merry before I set off for the vehicle and essentials tomorrow.

Friday 9th October

Got up a bit later than I thought today, Irfan surprised me last night, I knew he liked a drink but had no idea that he toked the weed too, I purposely did not offer him any because I was not sure if his religion frowned on it. I suppose that was me being ignorant because although I knew Islam would not tolerate anything that harms the body, I really had no idea about Hinduism, anyway after my second joint he looked at me and called me a tight git and was I intending on sharing the spliff, I was pleasantly surprised and offered it to him and told him that he could help himself to my dwindling supply. We had a brilliant night getting smashed, there was an awkward silence when he asked if I had a wife or kids, I have been out for over 25 years and it was nothing for me to admit I was gay but I could see the shock/surprise on his face, after a few minutes he smiled and explained that homosexuality was not really a big issue in his religion although still frowned upon plus it was the 21st century and he had no problems with it personally, to which he followed on by asking me if I had a partner before the end of the world. As I said earlier I knew Irfans character and he was not one to judge. I got my shit together after a strong cup of tea headed off to town in the crappy car, I did not mind leaving this piece of crap to its own fate at the industrial estate, I got the clothes Irfan needed and a few things for myself in town and packed them in the car to head out and get the vehicle. I was pleasantly surprised at the choice of luxury mobile homes, although most of us were living hand to mouth, there must have been a decent percentage of the population with money to burn, no doubt senior protection officers and other government flunkies plus of course big American and Chinese businesses that have effectively asset-stripped our country since leaving the EU. I know Boris feckin Johnson is long dead having killed himself in prison after he and several cabinet ministers were arrested and convicted of insider trading but the bastard still had a lot to answer for. Anyway, I chose a top of the range model with all the latest gadgets plus a wood-burning stove and with a back rack that held two electric motorbikes. This thing was brand spanking new and the cost was well over £400,000 to buy, the manuals were all there in the glove compartment and they stated the first charge would take four hours but after that, it could be achieved in 20 mins. I had a vehicle from here before and knew where the charging points were, first though I had to fetch the portable charger to give the vehicle enough life to move it there. I now had four hours plus to kill so headed back into town for what would be my last look at the city I called home. It seemed so long ago now that it all fell to pieces and as I walked along Morledge I noticed that the soldiers who had tried to put up a fight in the very early days were still here but now they were just pure white bones sticking out of shredded cloth no doubt picked clean by whatever wild animals inhabited the city now. I headed to

Tesco to get a frozen pasty, there were plenty of shops around with microwaves and all the city Centre was powered so I decided to take my heated food and a bottle of Dr Peppers to the gentrified waterfront overlooking the Derwent. I sat down and just chilled for a bit, it seemed odd to be alone here as the place was usually full of people taking in the serenity of it all. If I closed my eyes I could imagine that nothing had changed. I suddenly became sad and decided to leave this dead place and walk back to the industrial estate. I still had two hours to kill so I decided to clean the inside of the camper, it was brand new but over the last few months, the dust had accumulated. I just needed something to keep my mind occupied, part of me was dreading Wales but also there was a part that was excited at seeing the people that had become friends. I also knew from the increase in pain that this would be my last journey of any significance. I have tried denying what is happening but the weight loss and pain made it glaringly clear that I was not long for this world. By the time I had finished cleaning the camper was fully charged and good for well over 200 miles. There was one more stop I wanted to make before heading back to Irfan and that was to get as many laptops/hard drives and USB/micro sd cards as I could manage for David who ran the market garden/farm in Wales. I don't think I will be exchanging for much weed this time as I think I have a few weeks left alive maximum. Don't get me wrong, this illness will not take me, there is no way I am going to fight it out to my last breath. I had the necessary medication to fall asleep and not wake up and I knew from professionals that it would be painless.

Saturday 10th October

I managed to get plenty of electronics and digital storage yesterday and I was pleased with the haul when I got back, Irfan had prepared another great meal and we discussed our plans, we decided to head out first thing today and by 10 am we had locked up the house and headed for the M42 west. I had travelled this road a few times and knew it was clear, I think the only hold up we should have is if we come across a horde of infected. Irfan wound down his window and stuck his head out, I could not stop smiling because max did the same when he was cooped up for hours inside, obviously, max did not wind the window down but you know what I mean, we decided not to do the whole journey in one day because as soon as we get to wales Irfan fully expected to be confined for a few days whilst tests were taken. Once we bypassed Birmingham we decided to stop for some food on the M6, the day was cold but none the less a beautiful day and Irfan was amazing and delivered up another great vegetarian feast. After lunch we decided to head straight to St David because even though he was elated at moving on he found the emptiness of it all soul-destroying, the rest of the journey was no problem and we reached St David's by early evening, I knew the two guys on the main barricade and got out to greet them, after a small conversation in which I mentioned Irfan's unique position, the guard radioed through and within ten minutes our camper was surrounded by armed soldiers, I personally thought it was overkill but I realised that they needed to secure Irfan and to run tests. I did not need to explain anything to Irfan and he just smiled and assured we would meet up again soon. After they took Irfan and after I was examined by medical staff I was released. I was now at another loss, I had nowhere to live but judging on the number of people I have seen that would not be a problem, the streets were far from deserted but it was obvious that most of the population had moved into the Islands. I arrived at Sue and Ian's and Sue answered the door, I had never received such a true hug as the one I got and I could see tears in her eyes. I asked about Ian and Sue explained he had been on Island clearing duties for the last week but he was fine. Sue also explained she was pregnant and they had decided to stay in St David's because the mainland still needed nurses to tend to the ill and injured. I asked Sue if I could kip there until I found somewhere to live, she smiled at this and went into a draw and picked up some keys which she threw to me, she told me that they had kept my original flat for me to return. She did invite me and Max to stay over for dinner or the night if we wanted. I decided that we would stay here tonight and get my shit together tomorrow.

Sunday 11th October

Had an amazing night with Sue, I got shitfaced but Sue had to hold back on her intake because of her condition. I left her earlier getting ready for work and headed towards the flat, it was strange entering the place I used to call home with Jono, got to admit that a few tears escaped my eyes but happy tears because of the memories we made here. Max ran straight past me and to his bed that we got from a local pet shop. The poor guy was a mix of shattered and excited and closed his eyes and went straight to sleep. I left Max in the flat and headed to the hospital to see how fast my illness had progressed. I arrived at the hospital within the hour and it was easy enough to get an immediate appointment with one of the few DR'S left here, as most had followed the majority to the islands. I was pleased to see the DR was one of the ones I have met before and he knew my issues. After a brief examination and taking some blood he explained that results may take two weeks because most staff had moved to the Islands but he felt that my illness had spread rapidly and he could only offer pain relief. He was telling me basically what I knew as my body had informed me weeks ago things were getting worse, I know I said I did not want to come back St David's but I realise that in the weeks left to me I can say goodbye to some of the best people I have ever had the fortune to meet. I sat down and wrote a list of people it was important to see and planned another road trip for me and Max.

Monday 12th October

Went back to Sue's last night to tell her of my plans to drive to my sisters in Llannefydd and visit others along the way, she knew straight away that I was saying my goodbyes and I could see the tears in her eyes, after she gave me a massive hug me and Max headed out this morning for Llannefydd with a couple of stops on the way. The day was horrid, torrential rain but there should be no problems, First, we headed to Dave's farm/market garden because I had all the tech from the city for him plus I wanted to catch up with him and to see how Stephen, the guy I discovered in Swansea was doing. We made good time and arrived around 11am, Dave came to the main gate and gave me a massive smile. I pulled up in the drive and shook Dave's hand and out of the corner of my eye I saw Stephen running from the house, he gave me a bear hug but the fecker did not know his own strength and I was winded. We all went inside for a cuppa and a chat. It was good to see them both and the transformation of Stephen was incredible, he was well dressed in casuals and had put on some weight, he was so excited that he was now learning to read and write thanks, Dave, I knew he would fit in here and I am so pleased he had settled so well. After much catching up I asked Stephen if he could help me grab a few things from the camper. We had unloaded all the tech and took it in the house and Dave's face was a picture of smiles, he was not prepared to risk going to the cities himself and was pleased with anything tech that people bought back, even the Army referred to him now if they wanted anything in way of entertainment. I was invited to stay the night and Dave mentioned he had a bottle of single malt to break open plus all the weed I could smoke and as much as I can carry to take with me. The night went really well and everyone got really smashed, the only downer was when Dave asked me how my illness was going, I had to be honest and explain that this was my farewell tour (my humour had stayed with me throughout the whole almost demise of humanity) Dave took it well but Stephen burst into tears and hugged me, I know I should be thinking of me but I was just glad Stephen had found a place where he was respected and cared for, even loved. I did ask one favour though, I told him that others had said they would arrange for me to be buried with Jono in the cemetery but even though I loved Jono, I had not known him that long and just thought it odd. I asked outright if I could be buried in his top field. He agreed straight away and Stephen promised to lay flowers every week for me, I thought I would be scared of dying but I have always known it was a perfectly normal part of life and I had no religion so I was not concerned with heaven and hell. When I die I fully expect to cease to exist and the body was just a waste product. Don't get me wrong, people who believe in something are usually good until they become extremist and learn to hate others in the name of their gods. My philosophy has always been, give a man a fish and he eats, give the same man religion and the poor bastard will starve to death praying for a fish. Around 2ish we all retired for the night.

Tuesday 13th October

Did not get up until well gone noon and my head was hurting bigtime, Even after a good breakfast/lunch I was still feeling the effects and Dave noticed and told me to go back to bed and stay another night. I woke up around 5pm to the smell of chicken. I felt so tired still but knew I had to get up, I decided not to use the pain relief in case it subdued me too much but had to use some weed to help me out of bed. I put on my smiliest face and went to join Dave and Stephen. I had to smile when I entered the kitchen, Stephen and Max were rolling on the floor together whilst poor Dave was trying to get the meal ready, I had thought of Max's future and I assumed that Ian and Sue would take him but seeing him with Stephen made me think twice. I decided not to mention Max yet because there was no way I was letting him go until the very end. We all sat down to a nice meal and afterwards Dave had picked out a box set to start watching, no problem there because if it was good I could shove a copy on a stick and watch it via laptop later. The meal was amazing and I and Stephen washed up before I took Max out for a walk. The rest of the evening was very mellow and Stephen went off to bed which gave me the chance to talk to Dave about the possibility of Max staying when the time came. Dave was more than happy to let Stephen have him and said it may give him a bit more maturity caring for Max. We chatted for a couple of hours or so and both went off to bed around 10pm.

Wednesday 14th October

I felt totally rested this morning and actually woke up pain-free, which was becoming a rarity. After a nice brekkie, we said our goodbyes but promised to stop by on the way back. The day was cold but bright and we made good time arriving in Llannefydd by lunchtime. I knew today was going to be emotional because it would be the last time I would ever see my sister and her family, as soon as I got to Wendy's house the door opened and I got a massive hug from my niece Keeley. Wendy has always been pretty astute and as soon as I entered the kitchen she came over and after a hug asked if I had come to say a final goodbye, I knew I was feeling drained but had no idea how I looked to others but I guess My illness showed big-time now. I will not go into the details of the rest of the day, needless to say, it was emotional though. I stayed overnight and had what will be my last home-cooked meal as I had decided that on my way back after dropping Max off at Dave's that I would pull up in a layby and take the meds that would enable me to enter the eternal sleep, lol just read that and it's a poncy way of saying I'm going to end my life. We arrived at Dave's by mid-afternoon and I spoke to him about my plans and taking Max, he did make me agree to stay over for one more massive session and to be fair I was not reluctant in agreeing because it would be the last time in eternity that I could get out my face, people reading this in the future (if any) may think I am irresponsible and they would be right, not a cat in hells chance I am going to be a martyr to my pain, which is becoming a lot worse. I set off very early this morning and although my mind was made up I could not shake the feeling that I was abandoning Max but there was no way I was leaving him in the vehicle while I passed. I found a quiet lane on the way to St David and pulled over, I am not a courageous man and know that if I hesitate I may back down even though my future holds nothing but pain. I took out the medication I have had for a while now and filled the syringe, my letters in the flat will be found and the people I love and care for will get to read how much I loved them. I do not envy the living and their future. I only hope they get to live in tranquil and peaceful times without all the baggage of the past weighing them down, but society has a way of repeating mistakes, I think it is solely a human trait not to learn from our fuck ups. Nothing else for it now except to administer the meds. This is the scariest thing ever and I want to leave with some profound words but Goodbye is the only one I can think of.

Friday 23rd October

Hi, Sue here, I promised Mark that I would continue with this diary/log and I will try to update as often as possible. We buried Mark at Dave's farm in an outlying field, the send-off was what Mark would have wanted and was a celebration of his life, I and many others could not stop the tears when Stephen (who Mark had found in Swansea) read a letter he had written himself (not bad for a man who a few short weeks ago could not read. I had not known Mark long but we hit it off straight away but even I was surprised at the love from some of the people he had rescued personally.

Sunday 25th July 2027

Well so much for my monthly update, really sorry about that but my excuses are valid. I and Ian are now proud parents of a much loved new young son Jono and a three-month-old Shih Tzu called Kempy, Dave from the farm was given a female of the breed who was very near death when found in January, anyhoo Max did the dirty and is now also a proud father of six. I have been working almost right through the pregnancy and I am one of the few nurses left on the mainland still so I get to hear quite a lot of the office gossip. People no longer turn if bitten by the infected although the survival rate for a bite was still low some people did survive, I believe the research was based on a man Mark found wondering one of the cities last year who had been bitten but survived. It is almost certain now that the infection/disease was caused by the rushed out a vaccine for the covid 19 back in 21. Covid 19 was actually the most benign of the Covid pandemics but to be fair it was the first pandemic in several generations and the politicians and scientist panicked and did not test the vaccine extensively before releasing it. Covid never did go away it only mutated and we became immune to the Global death toll but not the virus, year after year the toll crept up, we stopped the pretense after the first two years and in late 21 we stopped calling the high infection rate waves and referred to them as pandemics in their own rights due to the fast mutations of the original strain. On a very positive note, many scientists globally had survived (either through military service or highly sensitive work at secure locations) and were now working together without politics or the ideals of their leaders stopping them. This has resulted in many successful air evacs worldwide and great strides in research into the (un)dead. The infected dead are still numerous in the cities and the main arteries like the M1/M4/M5/M25 are virtually impassable in some places, the masses of bodies that mark wrote about have almost fused into one stinking very slow-moving mass. They are not a big issue though as you have at least a day's warning if one of the masses is near because of the smell and the black clouds of ravens and other carrion eater floating on the thermals that the masses create. There are now dozens of small towns and a few cities all over the island that are now safe communities from Southampton to Edinburgh. The army even has one of the nuclear power plants open in the south. It seems that the people who worked there at the start of infection last year had the sense to evacuate their families behind the high-security wall around the facility. Not that it was absolutely necessary to have nuclear energy because the wind turbines all over the country were working fine and in fact were being maintained by groups of navy engineers from several countries, I probably need to explain that last bit, during the last year many naval ships from all over the world have chosen the Irish and north sea as their new homes, The UK sent out messages of friendship and welcome once global communications had been re-established just after the new year and several thousands of ships had set course. Food was not the issue, all of the fields on the Islands and many in the mainland had been planted in plenty of time for a harvest this year. Even without the harvests, we would have been good on tinned goods for a while yet. Going to finish now because Jono needs feeding but looking forward to contributing to Marks diary again shortly.

Printed in Great Britain
by Amazon

60906875R00092